'I cannot see the f[...] sense their mounting panic. Then I hear it: a strange, indescribably eerie cry, half human, half animal. The men stop as if frozen. They whisper to each other. Then suddenly begin to move again . . . Branches slap us in the face. We stumble over roots, fall, scramble to our feet and plunge ahead again. Our lungs are burning. But we are unable to escape from the weird cry. It follows us, rising sometimes to a hysterical wail then sinking to a soft, sobbing moan. . . . The sound grows nearer. I cover my ears with my hands and peer wildly around. There is nothing but blackness, total, as dark as death itself.'

Also by Bill Linn in Sphere Books:
MISSING IN ACTION

Kambe Hai

BILL LINN

SPHERE BOOKS LIMITED

First published in Great Britain by
Sphere Books Ltd 1987
27 Wrights Lane, London W8 5TZ
Copyright 1987 by Bill Linn

The author would like to acknowledge his use of the Kelabit
song from Tom Harrisson's book, *World Within: A Borneo
Story*. The author has tried unsuccessfully to locate Tom
Harrisson in order to request permission to use this material.
He is also thankful for facts and information about Borneo
unearthed by explorers and writers, past and present,
especially Tom Harrisson, Wyn Sargent and W. R. Geddes.

The author thanks the Michigan (USA) Council for the Arts,
whose generous grant enabled him to complete the research
for, and writing of, this work.

TRADE
MARK

Printed and bound in Great Britain by
Cox & Wyman Ltd, Reading

Kambe Hai is the river devil. All men fear him.

He went over the great mountain up and up into high jungle,
  to the highest peak and there the sun came out.
He followed the ranges and went so strongly that the
  mountains rolled and swayed, because he went so swiftly
  homeward.
He went on and on, until he came to the rice-clearing of
  Burong-Siwang – his own land.
He came down the hill to the plain and came near to the edge
  of the village.
He called out aloud and shouted for his father – 'Are you
  there, father, in the village, for Balang Lipang has arrived,
  he has fought with Tokud Udan.'
All the villagers, his father, his mother, came running out of
  the house and down the ladder to greet Balang Lipang.
'You have returned, son! Where did you go? You have been
  very long, these days I have waited for you, a long time –
  where have you travelled so far?'
I have been around and about, father. I have reached the land
  of Tokud Udan, and fought with him three months. I have
  got his head and so now I return . . .'

Kelabit song, recorded and translated
by Tom Harrisson in *World Within: A Borneo Story*

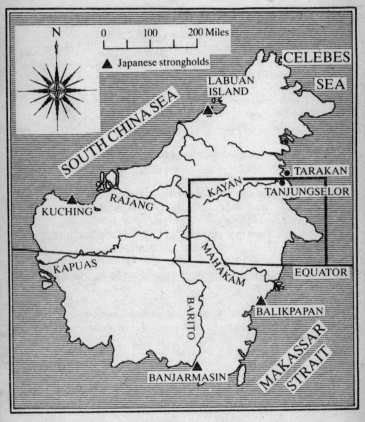

BORNEO IN 1944

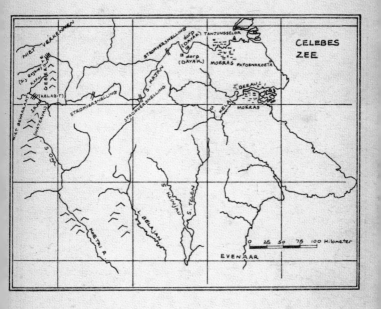

I

We are in a small boat going slowly up a river called the Kayan. It is early morning and steam is rising from the water, making the air shimmer, so that the insects that hover just above the surface seem to be dancing like motes of dust. There are four of us, myself, Montgomery, who is a buck sergeant, and Nance and Johnson – Nance and Johnson are privates. The boat we are on is piloted by one of the Malays; it moves slowly in the water which is brownish in colour and choked by thick weeds. The boat has a motor that makes a steady *put-put* which echoes loudly up and down the river. The river itself cuts a kind of canyon in the forest which is made up of tall trees and vines. We can see the trunks of the trees, black and very straight and with almost no branches until the top where suddenly there is an umbrella of foliage. Vines hang down from these branches, some over a hundred feet long. The vines form a green curtain and behind this there is nothing but blackness – a total blackness, blacker than the darkest night. Sometimes a monkey comes out of this darkness and hangs on one of the vines and peers at us. The monkeys have big, saucer-shaped eyes, and they are a funny tan colour, almost beige, and although we've all – Johnson, Nance, Montgomery and I – seen a lot of monkeys before, we've never seen monkeys like these.

Nobody is saying very much because we're all worried. The boat we're on leaks and we don't trust the man who is guiding us. We don't trust the jungle and we worry about the Japs who are out there somewhere, waiting and watching. In a war you learn not to trust anyone much because it doesn't pay. But it is the place that makes us really spooky. On the river there is

1

dead silence except for the *put-put* of the engine and now and then the screech from a monkey, but we can hear a sort of hum coming from the forest. It is low and indistinct, and it is unsettling all of us. Sometimes there are screams which sound almost human. Montgomery says they are made by the monkeys. Nance believes this, but Johnson doesn't – Johnson is the suspicious type, and I watch as his eyes dart from side to side.

We've been travelling for three days now, ever since the landing craft put us ashore on the beach at 2° 55′ north and 117° 59′ east near a place called Tanjungselor on the east coast of the Jap-occupied island of Borneo. The contact met us there and arranged for the boat and the guide. Then we started up the river. We didn't trust the contact – he was a thin, tubercular-looking Chinese who has worked for the Dutch for almost twenty years. We don't trust orientals – maybe it is because of Pearl Harbor and maybe it is because I'm the only one among the four of us who has ever known an oriental except to shoot at him – but we don't trust them. Montgomery wanted to kill this one—

'If we let him go, Captain, he'll tell the Nips. He's probably a double agent.'

Montgomery is from Tulsa and before he enlisted he worked on an oil rig. He's big and he's strong but he's not very smart, and he thinks the best way to win the war is to kill all orientals. Nance and Johnson are probably not sure. I don't know either of them well enough yet to come to any conclusions about them. They were assigned to the mission on the boat coming over from the Solomons, and I haven't spent enough time with them to be able to figure them out. Johnson is from Murfreesboro, Tennessee. He's a hillbilly and his teeth are bad, and he smells like whisky, although where he's getting it from I don't know. Nance is from Newark, New Jersey. He doesn't like Montgomery much and he likes Johnson less.

Up ahead we can see a place where the river starts to widen out a bit, and the Malay signals with his hand that we should go back inside, under the awning that covers the centre of the boat. We do this and crouch down low, so we're concealed in the shadows cast by the sides of the boat, and watch as we slide past half a dozen huts that line the edge of the river. The huts are supported by stilts, and some Malays are sitting in the doorways, fishing. They are about twenty feet above us, and we know that if they look hard they will be able to see us, but there is nothing much we can do about this. I see Montgomery's hands tighten around the stock of his rifle, and I tell him, with a shake of my head, that killing all the natives on the Kayan River won't do any good – that it's not the natives we have to worry about anyway but the Japs. I don't say all of this but he seems to understand, and I can see him remove his finger from the trigger, and I hear him snap the safety catch back on, but he doesn't put the gun down.

Nance and Johnson stare at the people. Neither of them has ever seen anything like this before.

Then we are past the village and the river narrows again, and the trees are overhead and it's very dark. I crawl out from under the awning and make a gesture to the Malay, asking with my hand if it's OK for the others to come out. He nods.

Johnson lights a cigarette and offers Montgomery one. I notice that he doesn't offer Nance one, so to balance things I hold out my own pack, and Nance reaches over and takes a cigarette. I hand him my box of matches and watch as he strikes one. We're moving slowly and there's no breeze so he doesn't need to protect the flame, but he makes a cup of his hands until the cigarette is lighted then tosses the match into the stream. His hands are large, with long, slender fingers. His skin is very dark – even darker than the Malay's – but the palms are much lighter. I've always wondered why that is so – why the palms of the hands and the soles of the feet are light on Negroes while the rest of their skin is dark. I speculate about it for the hundredth time. Maybe it's because of the sun, I think. That would make sense; pigment would be located on the surfaces of the body that need protection. The thought seems logical and I'm pleased that it has occurred to me. It tells me that I'm still thinking, that I'm not too blown away by the mission and the strangeness of the place to be a little detached.

There is a sudden screech behind me and I whirl around in time to see a large monkey, down almost on the bank of the river, screaming at us. Montgomery says 'Goddamn Jap monkey' and picks up one of the rusty bottle caps that litter the floor of the boat and throws it at the monkey. The animal jumps out of the way; then, after we have swept past, it reappears and leans out over the river to watch us go, scolding us with a final, defiant screech.

Suddenly we are in a wider part of the river again, and the

3

sunlight floods over us, bouncing off the water and blinding us. I shut my eyes, and then I hear the Malay say something and I try to see what he means but the sunlight is too bright and I can't.

'He wants us back down inside, Captain,' says Nance, and we scramble under the awning again and squat down. In the darkness I can see again and notice that the river has widened out into a small lake, and that there are more of the houses on stilts. They seem to cover an entire side of the lake shore, and the people in them have all come out to watch the boat go past.

Two canoes shoot out from beneath the houses and start to follow us. Each canoe is filled with a dozen men, and they paddle fast and start to gain on us. I say 'Faster' to the Malay even though I know he doesn't know the word. But he seems to understand, because he moves the throttle forward and our speed increases.

The canoes keep gaining on us though. Their paddles flash in the sun, and there is a small, white-capped wave at the prow of each. We watch as they come steadily closer. Now we can see the men rowing them more clearly. They have the high cheekbones and slanted eyes of orientals, but their skin is darker. It occurs to me that they resemble American Indians.

Now the canoes are only about thirty yards back, and I look at the men in them again. They seem to be smaller than we are, but I can't tell for certain because they are kneeling. The Malay has his attention focused on the river, but every once in a while he turns his head to look at the canoes. When he does so I notice a new expression on his face; it takes me a few minutes to realize that it's fear. He looks at me and says something that I can't hear because of the *put-put* of the motor which has grown louder.

'He's saying "Dayak," Captain,' says Nance. 'I think he's trying to tell us that these people are Dayaks.'

One of the canoes is a little ahead of the other now, and two men in it raise long tubes to their mouths. Now the Malay is really scared and crouches down.

Then they come – small, almost like insects, only flying much faster than any insect ever flies. They whizz over our heads and some of them hit the poles that support the awning and stick there, like darts in a board.

The other canoe moves closer now, and more men raise pipes to their mouths and the air is filled with the things. They

4

make a humming sound as they go overhead. Then I hear a click and I know that Montgomery has taken the safety catch off his rifle, and I know what's going to happen next, only this time I don't stop him.

There's a crack, and one of the Dayaks reels and falls backward into the water with a splash. But the other men in the canoe don't even look surprised, and it keeps on coming and the darts keep whizzing over our heads. Then there are two more shots and two more men fall into the water, but the canoes keep coming.

'Shoot for the prow!' I shout. 'Close to the waterline!'

There are three more cracks in quick succession, and suddenly there is a hole big enough to put your hand through in the prow of the closest canoe, and it slows down and begins to sink into the river.

The other canoe veers off, and Montgomery fires twice more; two large holes appear in its side and it starts to sink as well. Now Montgomery starts firing at the Dayaks in the water.

'Save the bullets,' I say. 'You don't need target practice.'

We turn our heads and watch as the Dayaks swim towards the shore; then there is a bend in the river and they have vanished and all there is are the trees and the vines and the *put-put* of our motor.

'Goddamn!' says Johnson. Montgomery looks at me and shakes his head.

The Malay has straightened up again. He looks towards us and smiles, showing a set of white, sharp-looking teeth.

Johnson stands up and starts to pull a dart out of one of the wooden poles that hold up the awning.

'If you prick yourself, you'll be stiff as a board inside of thirty seconds,' I say, but he keeps pulling at the thing. When he has it out he holds it up for everybody to see. It's about half as long as a finger and has three tiny feathered fins and a point like a needle. The point is stained dark red.

'The tip is coated with poison made from a mixture of a half dozen kinds of snake venom,' I tell him. 'The poison goes straight to the central nervous system. Then the muscles that work the diaphragm freeze and you suffocate.'

'Doesn't hardly look much different than one of the darts the boys play with in the game room on the ship,' Johnson says. 'Thing like that would hardly draw blood.'

'They don't want to draw blood,' I say. 'They want to keep it all in the body.'

5

'Why's that?' Johnson asks, still examining the dart.

'They drink it,' I say.

We travel through the afternoon. The sun, high overhead, bounces light off the river that stabs us in the eyes. Sometimes we doze, only to wake sweating like pigs.

Johnson and Montgomery play gin rummy. Montgomery is not very good and Johnson wins most of the time. They gamble for cigarettes and pretty soon Montgomery gets angry and quits. I watch Nance. He is sitting alone towards the front of the boat, staring at the forest as we glide past. I wonder what he is thinking – what kind of a man he is. Montgomery, I understand. Everything about him is on the surface. I know what will make him fight, what he's afraid of. He's the kind of soldier officers like: in a tough situation he'll follow orders and he won't ask many questions.

Johnson is an altogether different proposition. I can't depend on his doing what I want him to do. Johnson has it all figured out: he knows that the world is made up of guys who give orders and other guys who obey them. He also knows that he belongs in the latter category – luck and the fact that his father was a hillbilly who never went beyond the sixth grade have put him there. He doesn't much like things this way, but he's smart enough to try to hide his feelings. For him the game plan is very simple – he doesn't much care who wins or loses, he just intends to survive, and he will make damned certain that he doesn't risk his neck doing what I want him to do.

Nance seems to be a lot more sensitive than the other two. He keeps to himself and he doesn't say much. Once or twice I've noticed him studying Johnson. I think he has Johnson pegged. He hasn't decided about Montgomery yet.

The boat is going through shadow now. The river is narrow and the trees on both sides lean over it so that the sky is almost hidden. The water is still brown but it does not seem to be so choked with weeds as before, and I have a hunch it's a little deeper here. Once or twice I've seen fish break the surface, going after insects. They look like carp – fat and silver-grey. Old logs line the river-banks close to the shore. Sometimes they move a little; the ones that move are crocodiles. The information officer told me they sometimes reach twenty feet. He said we would find them mostly in the swamps near the coast, but already we're at least seventy-five miles inland and there seem to be more of them with each mile we cover.

According to the map, we won't run into any more villages for a while, but the map can't be too accurate. It's an old one, made by a Dutchman who traded on this river thirty years ago. All the other maps exist only in the heads of the natives.

The mosquitoes are biting. They're bigger than any I've ever seen before, and they don't seem to be bothered much by the insect repellent we're using. Borneo is filled with malaria; even the monkeys have it. The chances are fifty-fifty we'll get it, but it won't kill us – not unless it turns into blackwater fever.

Suddenly, the river bends to the north and the current speeds up. The Malay moves the throttle forward a few notches to try to keep up our speed. Towards the coast the current was slow, but the closer to the mountains we get, the faster it will be. We'll hit rapids but not for two more days – or at least that's what the Dutchman's map says.

The hum from the forest seems to have grown louder – probably that's because the river is narrower here and we're closer to the shore. I keep trying to see beyond the trunks of the trees and the vines hanging down between them, but I can see nothing but shadows. The trees are so thick that it's inconceivable that a man could get through, but the Japs are out there somewhere in the forest right now – a column of them, at least two hundred strong. Intelligence has been intercepting their reports for a month now, and we know that they're going after him – that's why I'm on this river now. We have to get to him first.

Now we can see the sun. It's dead ahead of us so that the river seems to be running straight into it. The boat has slowed some but is still moving steadily. The water is as smooth as glass, and the ripples made by the boat make a perfect 'V'. We see more monkeys – these are bigger than the monkeys with the saucer eyes. They hang in the branches and stare at us then suddenly whirl and swing off into the shadows of the forest.

There is a new noise – a mechanical buzz somewhere behind us and high up. Instantly everybody moves under the awning, and I get out my field glasses.

There are two of them and they're still about a mile back. I watch as they grow bigger. I can see the rising sun on the underside of the wings. They fly over the boat and their shadows follow a second later, flitting over the water like giant birds. They probably didn't see us – they were too high and going too fast – but we can't be sure.

The sun is only half visible now, a crimson ball of fire sunk part way behind the western horizon. Everything is quiet. From somewhere nearby we hear the soft 'caw-caw' of a bird. Then the sun is gone and it's dark; the moon, behind us, is only a dull yellow-orange platter that throws no light. Mosquitoes buzz around us, and every minute or so we have to slap our faces or our arms. When we do this we usually kill half a dozen. We can feel the lumps from their bites.

'This stuff they gave us doesn't do any damn good,' says Montgomery. 'What the hell they bother for? We may as well be coating ourselves with sugar.'

He goes to join Johnson and Nance under the awning. There is a net spread around it but somehow the mosquitoes get through. Still, it's better in there.

Fish are jumping, and sometimes we hear a big splash near the shore that means a croc has dived in to go hunting. The forest is blacker than ever, and now the hum that comes from it is filled with other noises. Some sound like the screeches of monkeys, but mixed in are new sounds which I can't hear clearly enough to identify. And above everything, drowning it all out, is the hum of the insects which seems to grow louder each minute.

'You think the Japs are out there? You think they're looking for us?'

It's Nance. He's come out from under the awning and stands at my elbow, smoking a cigarette.

'We don't have to worry until it gets light again,' I say.

Nance chucks the glowing stub of his cigarette into the river, and something big whizzes by our faces, circles, then whizzes past us again. It makes a high-pitched, chirping sound.

'Bats,' says Nance.

We're quiet then for a while. I can feel Nance standing there, breathing in the darkness, but I can't see his face clearly. The jungle slides past in a blur, and beneath us the river glints like melted chocolate in the pale moonlight.

'Why do they want this man, Captain? Why are they sendin' us all this way for him?' Then, as if to answer his own question – 'Guess he must be pretty important all right.'

'He's a senator's son,' I say, then chuckle at my joke, but Nance isn't in a joking mood. There are too many mosquitoes and it's too hot and he's too worried.

'Ain't no senator's son going to be stuck in a place like this in the middle of a war, Captain. Why don't you tell me who we're goin' to get? What difference does it make? Ain't nobody I can tell.'

But we both know that isn't true. We know what will happen if the Japs catch us, so I don't say anything and after a few minutes Nance changes the subject.

'This place is hot, Captain. I been in hot places before – once spent a whole summer in Savannah – but that ain't nowhere near as hot as this place. It's almost midnight and still it ain't let up.'

'It'll get cooler later, when we get up in the mountains,' I reply.

Nance doesn't say any more, and a minute later he goes back under the awning to join Montgomery and Johnson. Johnson is stretched out and snoring like a pig. Montgomery is curled up with his back braced against a crate. He's got his rifle resting across his knees. I hope that nobody wakes him up too quick because he's liable to come up firing.

For a while I watch the river then take out a pack of cigarettes and light one. I'm tired of smoking but the smoke seems to keep the mosquitoes away. I'm thinking of the orders they gave me before we left the Solomons. They were clear enough: 'Bring out a priest who has been living at the headwaters of the Kayan for almost ten years among a people called the Kelabit. The priest has been radioing out information about the movements of the troops occupying the island, and now the Japs are looking for him. Under no circumstances can we let him fall into their hands.'

There are voices behind me under the awning. Johnson and Montgomery are playing gin rummy again. Johnson has turned on the flashlight and a huge cloud of insects has collected. I ask him if he wants to tell every mosquito on the island as well as any Jap who might be looking for us exactly where to find us, and he shuts the light off, saying something about Yankees as he does so.

Then it's quiet and dark again, and I think some more about what we have to do. The words of the intelligence service man come back to me – 'Speaks the Dayak language . . . has a lot of influence with the natives . . . Japs could use him against us.'

Somehow it doesn't all add up, but then I'm not sure it's supposed to. They only give you the minimum number of pieces that you need to have to play the game – no more – because that way, if you're caught, only you go. It's pragmatic even if it's not very satisfying. I wonder what my colleagues at the university would say about that if they heard it? Somebody would quote Tennyson:

> 'Theirs not to make reply,
> Theirs not to reason why,
> Theirs but to do and die.'

That would be Brady. He would be wearing a tweed sports jacket, and there would be a cynical smile on his thin lips. Right now he's probably reading Pater to one of his classes, and half the students are sleeping. Brady is an intellectual snob. It's too easy to be a cynic. This is a war, and in a war you have to believe that the guy who's giving orders knows what he's doing – otherwise nothing works.

The river narrows and the trees close overhead again, and the hum of mosquitoes is almost deafening. I hear the cries again. They sound almost human. Behind those trees another war is going on. It's the same everywhere.

I go under the awning and find a place to lie down. I can smell the others now. The odour of their bodies mingles with the smells of the jungle and the river. I'd better get used to it – it will be a long time before any of us gets a chance to take a bath.

II

Just before dawn the insects stop singing for a few minutes. The silence wakens me. A peculiar grey light is filtering through the trees and everything is dripping wet. I crawl out from under the awning and stand on the deck. The *put-put* of the motor seems softer now and we are moving almost silently through water that appears to be absolutely still. The Malay is sitting by the steering wheel he has rigged up near the front of the boat, but he's hunched down as if he's half sleeping. We were moving when I went to sleep and we're moving now, but it seems impossible that he ran the motor all night – he had to sleep sometime.

We are very close to the forest now; not more than twenty yards separates us from the trees. The light is weak, but I think I can see something moving in the trees about thirty yards ahead of us; then, suddenly, it raises its head – it is large and almost human, the eyes sad, the expression lugubrious. Long red hair covers the head and arms.

'*Maias*!' says the Malay.

As we glide past, it turns to watch us then, using its hand-like paw as a cup, raises some water to its mouth.

Now we see more and more animals. They all seem to be coming down to the river to drink before the sun rises. There are countless monkeys – the beige ones with great saucer-shaped eyes, larger grey ones, and small brown ones with a dab of white at their chests. I see a herd of wild pigs, the tusks of the bulls curving fiercely past their snouts.

The river widens and along one side there is a swamp with dead trees and reeds. Three tiny deer are drinking in the water there, and they raise their heads to watch us pass.

11

Brighter light is starting to creep through the leaves, and all at once the top of the sun appears over the horizon behind us, shooting shafts of crimson over the trees.

Nance comes out from under the awning to watch. Montgomery and Johnson are still sleeping. Montgomery has his hand on the stock of his rifle; he probably slept like that all night.

We go to the rear of the boat where the Malay has a small stove supported on bricks, and Nance chucks in another piece of coal. Coals have been glowing inside the stove all night, and it is filled with fine white powder. We take some coffee from a bag, add it to a pot of water and bring it to a boil. The aroma rises and fills the air, seeming strangely out of place in the middle of the jungle.

The coffee is good and we sip it slowly. Then we eat some fruit and rice cakes, washing the food down with more coffee. By the time we have finished, Montgomery and Johnson have joined us. Neither of them looks like he spent a very comfortable night. Johnson smokes while he sips his coffee, alternating drags on his cigarette with loud slurps. Montgomery gorges himself on fruit. This will probably give him an attack of the runs, but I decide he'll have to discover it for himself: I don't feel like playing mother hen.

When everybody has finished eating we stretch out on the deck. The bugs have not started to bite yet and the air is as cool as it will ever be. The river is wide just here and it almost feels like there is a breeze. We shut our eyes and fall into a half sleep.

I wake with a start. A strange noise fills the air; it sounds like thunder and seems to be growing louder. I must have been hearing it for a long time, for I remember I was dreaming of a storm with lightning and thunder.

Nance is standing at the bow. When he sees me he points straight ahead. About a half mile upstream there is a fine mist above the water, and above that hangs a very low grey cloud that looks peculiar because the rest of the sky is completely cloudless. I know what it means without consulting my map: we have come to the first rapids. The Dutchman indicated this place with several lines running diagonally across the river. On the map it looked small and insignificant.

The Malay doesn't seem worried though. He pushes the throttle forward and we speed up a bit. Now we are about three hundred yards from the rapids and I can see them more clearly. The water is foaming and bubbling, as if it were boiling. The rapids are not steep but they are at least a quarter mile in length, and because of the mist hanging over them the trees beside the river are dripping, and there is a profusion of strange, brightly coloured flowers.

We enter the rapids and immediately the boat begins to buck like a horse. It makes slow progress, first raising its prow, then dipping down, then angling up again.

Slowly we climb through. We are all standing on the deck to watch what happens, soaking wet. The mist feels good – it's the first time we've been cool since we came to Borneo. Nance wipes the water off his face with his shirt, looks at me and laughs. Montgomery is standing on the other side of the awning, still holding his rifle, as if he might have to shoot the water any minute. Johnson is in the bow, in front of the Malay. I yell to him to move back because already I've seen the bow go under twice, but he acts like he doesn't hear me.

We are two-thirds of the way through the rapids now, and I'm beginning to think that they were not as bad as I had feared. The Malay evidently knows what he is doing. I look up at the cloud overhead. It's about a hundred feet above the water and completely obscures the sun. Ahead, a little past the place where the rapids end, the water glitters in sunlight, but here it is as if the day were overcast.

Now we are almost out of the rapids and I'm beginning to relax. I turn to Nance and start to say something when I hear a shout. The boat has taken a last, sudden dip headfirst, and the water is over the bow and Johnson is in the river.

We watch as, arms flailing, he is swept past us and down the rapids like a leaf. Montgomery wants the Malay to turn and follow him but the Malay won't do it; he swears at the Malay and tries to grab the wheel, but I stop him. If we try to turn here we'll flip over; nothing can be done until we are completely clear of the rapids.

Once we're beyond the white water the Malay swings the boat around, and then we are in the rapids again. This time we go much faster, almost leaping through the water. It occurs to me that there are rocks under all that foam, and if we hit one we'll be in the river with Johnson and the mission will be over.

Then we are past the rapids but still moving like a runaway horse. We can see Johnson about two hundred yards ahead; he is swimming slowly towards the shore on our right. He sees us and raises a hand and starts to tread water.

We're watching him and thinking he's pretty lucky when Nance points to a place about fifty yards to the left of Johnson, towards the centre of the river. I see what looks like an old log, then suddenly realize that if it was a log it would be moving downstream and not across the current. I grab Montgomery's arm and point. He raises his rifle, sights, and fires.

His first shot hits the water in front of the croc; the second seems to be on target, but the thing keeps going. He fires again and again but it keeps moving, not going any faster or any slower.

'The damn thing's like a tank!' Montgomery yells, firing once more.

Johnson has heard the shots and now he sees the croc too. He begins to swim towards the shore again, beating the water like a maniac. The croc is about fifteen yards from him now. It seems to have sunk down a little lower in the water, so that all we can see are the two bumps just behind its eyes and the tail, undulating back and forth smoothly. We're still twenty yards away and moving as fast as the motor can drive us. I take a rope and toss it towards Johnson. He grabs it and I start frantically reeling him in. The croc alters its course and moves towards him.

Suddenly Nance is at the bow of the boat. He's got something in his hand that looks like a big chunk of meat, and he leans back then heaves it towards the decreasing space between the croc and Johnson. Whatever it is hits the water with a splash; then there is a swirl and the croc has it, rolls over and vanishes under the water. A few seconds later Johnson scrambles aboard; then we all sit down with our backs against the bulwarks of the boat to catch our breath.

Johnson looks like a wet rat and is shaking like he has the palsy. Montgomery rests his rifle on his knees, looks at Johnson and just shakes his head. Nance is watching them both with a kind of amused detachment. I wonder whether he's thinking he should have let the croc get the red-neck bastard. The Malay shouts something towards us then starts to swing the boat around. When we're headed upstream again, he points to Johnson and then towards a long fishing pole which he has tied to one of the supports of the awning.

'What's Slant-eyes yakking about?' Montgomery asks.

'He wants Johnson to fish,' says Nance.

Montgomery looks confused.

'Nance fed that croc our supper for the next week,' I say. 'The Malay is complaining. He thinks that because Johnson caused all the trouble he should be the one to get us supper.'

Johnson is still shaking, but he manages to say 'Fuck him!'

The sun is beating down and the forest is quiet. Nothing can move in the heat. It feels like we are in a furnace. The Malay has found an old umbrella and sits under it, fanning himself as he guides the boat. Johnson and Montgomery have gone under the awning. I am sitting a little behind the Malay, in a place where a large crate throws some shadow. Nance is next to me. He has rigged the pole, baited it and dropped the hook into the water. He's been fishing for almost an hour and still hasn't caught a thing.

Johnson and Montgomery are under the awning. For a while they played gin rummy, but now they are sleeping again. I think Johnson is drunk but it's a mystery to me where he's getting the stuff. Montgomery carries his rifle everywhere he goes; now he is sleeping with his arm over it, as if it were his sweetheart.

It's late afternoon. The hum of the insects coming from the forest makes me drowsy, but each time I start to drop off my eyes pop open again.

Nance yells and jerks the rod back and a large fish appears near the surface of the water. He lifts it gingerly aboard and it flops around until he bangs it on the deck.

'How do you think it will taste?' I ask.

'Like catfish, Captain,' Nance says. 'Ever have catfish? You can taste the mud in their flesh.'

I say that sounds good and lean back and watch the sky pass overhead. It's very blue and behind us, to the west, I can see a few clouds. Somewhere out there, three thousand miles away, the Pacific Fleet is waiting. They will move to the Carolines and the Marianas then to the Philippines. Finally they will join up with MacArthur for the push towards Japan. Six months, a year at the most, and the war will be over and all of this will be only a memory. The thing to do is survive, that's all. Just to make it through. If it wasn't for this damned priest we'd be lying on the deck of a ship somewhere in the Solomons sunning ourselves and waiting for our next R and R. But you have to do what they tell you. A man doesn't have any choice. This mission is stupid, but if the priest has been helping us, I guess we owe it to him to get him out.

Suddenly there is a shot, then another. Nance and Johnson flatten themselves on the deck; Montgomery is kneeling at the bow, firing at something in the forest. There are three more shots, and now I can see movement among the shadows of the forest on our right. A bullet splinters one of the poles supporting the awning and it collapses. The Malay is crouched down low now, hiding behind a crate, but he keeps his hand on the throttle and we're still moving.

Then I see them – half a dozen Japs in tan uniforms, behind a big log about forty yards ahead of us, and what looks like a machine gun extending over the log. They will cut us to ribbons when we pass them. Montgomery has seen them too and is firing at them, but that only makes them crouch down lower. They can't see very well when they're low like that, but they won't have to see from there – all they'll have to do will be pull the trigger and we'll look like Swiss cheese.

We've got grenades stored in our gear, but the distance is still too great to use them effectively. The Malay starts to cut the engine and I crawl to the wheel and push the throttle forward again, yelling to Nance and Johnson to get the grenades ready. Now we are about thirty yards from the log, and I can see activity behind it. That means the Japs are getting ready to fire.

Johnson and Nance heave the grenades. The first two fall short, exploding in the river and raising a curtain of spray. There is a *rat-tat-tat* as the Japs open up with the machine gun, then the sound of bullets plunking into the wooden hull of the boat. There is one more explosion then the machine gun stops, and we glide past the log. More shots come but these are from lone snipers, far downstream. In a moment we have rounded a bend and the Japs are behind us.

Montgomery stands up and starts to take his rifle apart to clean it. I inspect the hull of the boat. It is peppered with holes, but these are above the waterline and will do little harm. Johnson and Nance join me.

'Who is the eagle-eye?' I ask, but neither of them answers.

'Nance, Captain,' says Montgomery, who has come over to look at the holes too. 'He winged it in there like Bob Feller.'

16

'They'll try again,' I say. 'Good thing we only used three grenades. It looks like we'll need the rest.'

'We better not count on grenades,' says Nance.

'What's wrong, hurt your arm?' I say, but he just shrugs and looks down at the holes. Johnson looks worried. I have a sudden suspicion and go back to inspect the pack in which grenades are stored: it's still full all right, but not with grenades. Now I know where Johnson has been keeping his whisky.

The sun is behind us now and we are making steady progress. Nance has taken over the wheel, and the Malay is grilling the fish. My mouth is watering, the aroma is so good. The jungle has begun to look different. The trees are the same – the same vines, the same impenetrable shadows – but now we can see hills and valleys instead of only the flat, featureless sea of trees. The river seems to be flowing faster. According to the Dutchman's map, there are rapids along here, but we haven't encountered any since that first set. The air is still warm, but it seems to be cooling a bit, especially now that the sun is sinking.

We eat just before sunset. The fish tastes delicious, and we wash it down with some special coffee the Malay has brought with him. There is chocolate mixed with the coffee beans, and it's bittersweet. Then we stretch out and watch the day die. The steady *put-put* of the boat echoes loudly in the stillness. Then there is a new sound. At first it sounds like distant rolling thunder and our eyes go towards the sky, but we can see nothing. Maybe there are planes up there, cruising through the gathering darkness. The sound is too loud and deep for fighters; perhaps a squadron of bombers, but there is no reason for bombers to be in Borneo.

We are still staring at the sky when the boat begins to tremble. There is white water all around us. Now we know what is making the thunder. The current in these rapids is stronger than in the first set, and the Malay is having trouble. We inch forward, stop, then move forward again. The river is very narrow here and the bank on either side not more than fifteen yards away from us.

The Malay races the motor, but it does no good; slowly, almost imperceptibly, we are losing the struggle. We veer and the current hits us broadside and for a moment we list and almost turn over; then suddenly we are whirled about and whipped headfirst downstream, shooting out into the quiet pool of the river below the rapids.

The Malay stops the motor and we all stand and look back upstream. Night has fallen, but even in the darkness we can see the foam.

We can't stay here. The Japs are only thirty miles back and they may be following the river upstream. If they catch us here, they will have us like a mouse in a trap.

The Malay has ropes coiled at the bow. We tie two to stanchions. Nance and I will head for the left bank, Montgomery and Johnson for the right. When we go over the side and slide into the water, its coldness and force shocks us. Johnson starts to flounder, but Montgomery is a strong swimmer and he pulls him along with him. By the time we reach the bank we've been carried nearly fifty yards downstream.

It's the first time we've been on land since we started up the river, and the feeling is eerie. The forest seems to be pressing in on us and the sounds coming from it are much louder.

We start to make our way upstream, but the going is slow. The trees come down to the edge of the river-bank, almost forming an impenetrable wall, and the bank itself is steep and slippery. Slowly, we move back towards the boat, slipping and sliding, sometimes holding onto the roots of trees, plunged into water up to our waists, at other times pressed flat against the trees and edging ourselves along with our backs to the stream.

It takes almost half an hour to reach a place parallel with the boat; then we move ahead thirty yards, swing the ropes around tree trunks and, using them as pulleys, slowly draw the boat towards us. Then we go through the same process again, the men on one bank staying behind to hold the boat even while the others take their rope about twenty yards upstream.

It is after midnight when we reach the top of the rapids, exhausted and covered with slime. We wade into the water then swim out a few yards from the shore to wash the slime off. Beyond, we can see the pale yellow moon reflected in the glistening surface of the water. The river is slow-moving here, and it is easy to keep our position. We swim over to the boat and climb aboard. Nance goes back to the river-bank and unties the last rope that is holding the boat against the current. The Malay guns the engine, and the boat begins to slide forward.

I watch as Nance is pulled through the water by Montgomery. He climbs on the deck and shivers. I go over to him and light a match. In its glow we can see a cluster of leeches on each of his arms. There are more on his ankles and feet. In all there must be twenty-five or thirty on him. We take turns burning them off with matches. When the flame hits the leech, it sizzles, curls up and drops off. Sometimes we burn Nance instead of the leeches. When this happens he curses.

We are moving steadily again. The surface of the river is smooth but the current is strong and the engine is working hard. Now the forest almost seems to be on top of us, and a sickening sweetness perfumes the air. Sometimes we pass close to great orchids which have twined themselves around the limbs of trees that overhang the water. Nance spots a python on one of these branches. We pass within a dozen feet of it and see its head, flat and nearly as wide as an automobile tyre. The heat has let up a bit but the mosquitoes are still ferocious. I smoke constantly; tobacco smoke seems to be the only effective repellant.

When dawn comes we are still moving. The Malay has run the motor all night. Now he appears to be dozing, but every once in a while he speeds the engine up a bit or alters our course so that we stay in the centre of the river, as far from the shore as possible. I can see mountains rising in the distance; they are covered with a green mat of trees, but they look rugged. Two birds appear about fifty yards upstream, directly ahead of us. They come on very fast, skimming so low that they almost touch the water. Just before they reach us their trajectory suddenly turns upward, and they zoom over our heads.

Now we begin to see animals again as they come down to the river to drink: innumerable monkeys, mostly small and dark brown, and once a deer, so tiny that it's almost like a toy. The air is noticeably cooler here, even for the first hours of day, and there aren't as many mosquitoes as before. I go back to put some coffee on the Malay's stove and am adding a piece of coal to the fire when I hear the Malay call out and twist around.

Directly ahead is a solid line of canoes, blockading the river from bank to bank. The men sitting in them have painted their faces white with red stripes on their cheeks. The Malay's face has the same scared look it had when the Dayaks chased us before, only this time his fear has turned to terror. As

19

Montgomery and Nance climb out from under the awning one of the canoes separates itself from the others and moves towards us.

'I can pot them from right here,' says Montgomery, and I hear a click as he releases the safety catch on his rifle.

In front of me, thirty yards upstream, are about a hundred men. I don't know the customs of this tribe, but to me these men look like a war party. If they are like the first group of Dayaks we met, a bullet from Montgomery's rifle will not have much effect on their mood. And even if we shoot our way past them, we still have to return when we come back downstream. I reach out and put my hand on his rifle, lowering the barrel.

The canoe glides smoothly towards us until it is about ten feet away; then the rowers feather their paddles and it turns and stops. A man at the front of the canoe stands up. His earlobes are grotesquely long, as if they have been stretched by some great weight, and protruding from the top of each ear is a tusk of bone that has been pushed through the cartilage. He says something to the Malay. I can see the Malay is having difficulty understanding the man, probably because he is so frightened. The man repeats himself then points upstream, towards the distant mountains. Now the Malay understands, and he turns and explains, half in gestures, half by words, that the war party wants us to follow them – that the 'man of God' – these are the words he uses – has sent them to meet us.

III

The canoes have been moving steadily through the water for almost six hours. The Malay has kept the engine at the same speed and the canoes have kept even with us, sometimes even surging ahead if there was a narrow place in the river to navigate. The river has begun to twist and turn like a road that is corkscrewing, and although we are hardly aware that we have been climbing, we are now in the mountains. The vegetation lining the river-bank is still thick and the forest is the same, but the sky has changed. Before it was always clear and sunny; now clouds, heavy with rain, hang just above the forest, obscuring the sun. The water in the river has lost some of its chocolate colour here, and sometimes we can see a few feet down into it.

We lie on the deck and doze while the boat chugs along. Montgomery and Johnson play cards, but Montgomery is tired of losing and quits after a few hands. Nance contents himself with watching the river. Sometimes he points things out to me – an animal we have never seen before or a brightly-coloured flower. This place excites him, he is like a kid at Coney Island. I ask him what his hometown is like.

'Newark, Captain – you want to know what Newark is like?' Then he chuckles. 'About four hundred thousand black people and fifty thousand Italians. The Italians own everything – the bars, the restaurants . . . they even own the garbage trucks. Newark is a pit, Captain.'

He looks back at the river again. I look for a trace of anger in his face, but there is none, only a kind of blankness, as if all feeling had been wiped away; then his eyes light up and he points again.

21

'There – see that, Captain? – that's the third one I've seen – they look like the monkeys we saw below, but up close they're different: the nose is more pointed and the tail longer.'

My eyes follow his finger and I see a dozen of the creatures, hanging high in a tree we are passing. They watch us like they were movie fans sitting in the balcony and we were part of the afternoon show. A small one – I guess it must be a baby – points at us and starts to leap up and down making a weird noise that sounds like laughter. Montgomery, who has been trying to sleep since he quit playing cards, opens his eyes and curses. He has his rifle in his hands as always, and I know he is itching to shoot the monkey who disturbed his sleep. Before we were stopped by the men in canoes he was worried but still rational; now, with each mile we go, he seems to become more and more unhinged. He cannot handle the idea that we are in the hands of these people, that they have us in their power. If we were engaged in a pitched battle with a dozen Jap soldiers he would probably be as cool as a cucumber – that kind of situation he understands – but this is something new, and he doesn't know how to react; and because he doesn't know what to do, he is frightened and wants to strike out.

The current suddenly increases, and ahead we can see more white water. I watch as the canoes navigate the rapids, the men paddling frantically. Then we are in the white water and the sound is deafening. Far ahead, I can see a place where the river widens out into a pool, almost forming a small lake, but between us and that place there lies at least a quarter mile of foaming, surging turbulence. The boat begins to toss wildly and we have to crouch down and grab onto the bulwarks to keep from being thrown overboard. The Malay is gripping the wheel grimly, but the power of the stream is too much for him, and he cannot keep the boat on an even keel. Then Nance is beside him, and together they hold the wheel steady and gradually we navigate our way through the rapids.

Foam and spray fill the air, so that it is almost impossible to see. Johnson loses his grip and slides towards the stern. The Malay's stove is knocked over, and I grab it to keep it from being swept overboard. There is a cough and a sputter: for a moment the engine almost conks out and we are swept backward. Then, with another sputter, it starts up again, and again we are climbing through the rapids.

When we finally reach the calm pool at the head of the

rapids, the canoes have spread themselves out in two parallel lines as if to form an escort. A man in the lead canoe signals, and we move on. Now the banks of the river are bare, and where the rushing water has cut a channel through it, the red earth is naked and raw-looking. Below, in the flatlands, the forest dominated, so that at times even the mud-filled water of the river seemed part of the vegetation. But here in the mountains the forest seems to have lost its dominating grip. The trees are still thick, but the forest does not overwhelm us, and occasionally there is an open place where the trees thin out into what might almost be called a savannah.

The engine must work much harder here, for we are constantly climbing and the force of the down-rushing current is strong. If a piece of paper or a chip of wood is thrown overboard, it vanishes in a second, whirled backward towards the lowlands. It is amazing that the men rowing the canoes have not tired, but their arms continue to rise and fall with the synchronized regularity of a well-oiled machine. Once they stop to eat what looks like dried meat, which they remove from leather pouches each has tied to a cord draped over one shoulder then wrapped around the waist, but that is only for fifteen minutes or so. They hold the pattern they formed at the head of the last rapids: two lines of canoes, the point canoe about twenty-five yards beyond our prow, the arms of the V angled towards the river-banks and extending forty yards behind us. Obviously they are doing this to protect us, from whom or what we don't know.

We round a bend and the river splits in two, one branch heading sharply north, the other easing off to the southwest. Between them lies a great, tree-covered bluff. A man in the lead canoe points towards the southern branch, and all head down it. I look off to the north: there the land seems to rise steeply and I can hear the faint roar of a rapids. The current in this branch of the river is weaker and our speed increases. The sun is behind us but still above the horizon. From its position, I can tell that there are not more than two or three hours of light left.

We reach a part of the river that is perfectly straight, almost like a canal. Trees lean over water that is so smooth it reflects the branches like a mirror. Now I notice that the men in the canoes are behaving differently. Some continue to row, but others hold small bows or pipe-like blowguns in their hands.

23

These men are peering towards the trees, as if looking for something. Each holds a small, round shield in his free hand.

The straight section of the river seems to go on and on. I cannot judge distance well on the water, but it seems we have been going straight for almost two miles when suddenly the air is filled with the hum of arrows and darts. The men in the canoes raise their shields, and we crouch down. The arrows continue to come at us, although we cannot see who is shooting them.

The river swerves to the east and the arrows stop. Johnson exhales and starts to stand up. I tell him to keep down. I am watching the men in the canoes and they are still holding their shields. Now their attention is focused on the river directly ahead of us. In a minute I see why, for a dozen canoes appear, seeming to slip magically out of the forest. The men in these canoes have faces painted white like the men who are escorting us. The intercepting canoes stay along the bank of the river, which is wide here, forming two parallel lines outside the V which is protecting us.

Then the battle begins again. The arrows and darts come in waves, like wind-driven rain. First the attackers loose a hail of arrows that the men in the escorting canoes block with their shields, then the hail is returned. The arrows are small, hardly more than two feet in length, and finned with green and brown feathers. They are frail-looking and seldom seem to draw blood, but when they do, I notice that the wounded quickly collapse – the arrows are probably tipped with the same poison as the darts used in the blowguns.

The battle rages for mile after mile. Perhaps a dozen men have been wounded. Suddenly the attackers on our right veer towards the escort canoes and ram into them. With shouts – the first sounds the fighters have made – the men in the canoes struggle hand to hand, using knives and short, red-tipped spears. Soon the river is filled with thrashing, struggling men. Knives flash in the sunlight and the water is stained red.

The battle is over quickly. The attackers are repulsed and they swim to the shore and quickly disappear into the forest. The men in our escort swim back to their canoes and crawl into them; some pull the corpses of dead enemies with them. Then it starts: using their long knives, the men in the canoes saw the heads off the corpses. When they have finished they dump the bodies overboard, where they sink from sight, and the heads

24

are meted out to the warriors who claimed the victims. They hang the heads from their belts, looping and knotting the long hair around the leather thongs that encircle their waists. After they have done this, the men pick up their paddles, and we resume our journey.

No one speaks for several minutes. Finally Montgomery says, 'Sweet Jesus!'

'I ain't never seen nothing like that before,' adds Johnson, shaking his head.

Nance is silent. We exchange a look but say nothing because there is nothing to say. For the first time we have had a glimpse of what lies beyond in the shadows of the forest.

Night has come and with it rain, falling in great, heavy drops that beat like hail on the awning of the boat. We are still moving at the same speed. The moon is obscured and the darkness is like a great blanket, covering all. Twice now the Malay has almost run the boat aground on the river-bank, and with each mile we cover, visibility is getting worse. The river twists and turns like a serpent. The men in the canoes know this river but the Malay is confused. I watch as he peers into the darkness, looking for the trees that mark the bank. He has put up an umbrella, but it does little good and he is soaked.

The others are sleeping. Under the awning it is fairly dry and the sound of the rain is soothing. The excitement of the day has tired them and they have collapsed into sleep. I am wondering about the man we will meet and the journey and the Japs. So far we have been lucky and things are on schedule, but our luck cannot last forever. We are in territory that is blank on most maps. The closest supporting forces are a thousand miles away, and the jungle and hostile natives and the Japs are all waiting to get us. I think of my wife back in Madison, of my two kids who probably won't know me when I return – if I ever do return. I wonder what my wife is doing right now and what the kids look like: one was two and the other four when I last saw them. The little one was still teething. Everybody said he looked like his mother, but he has my eyes – the eyes of someone who is a little bored with the world and always will be, the eyes of a scholar who prefers books to life.

The rain has got worse and a wind risen. Now water is being blown straight into our faces. For a few minutes more the

Malay runs the engine; then he shuts it off, ties up to the bank, and without saying anything crawls under the awning, wraps a blanket around himself, and in a minute is asleep. I wait, wondering what is going to happen. If visibility was poor before, now it is absolutely zero. Everything is reduced to sound – the splatter of great raindrops as they pepper the surface of the river.

I hear soft hoots like an owl makes. Once, twice . . . then they are repeated. They are coming from different sides of the river. I guess our escort party has taken refuge in the forest; under the trees it would be wet, but still they would be sheltered from the worst of the storm. Once more the cries come; then there is only the sound of the raindrops. The rain increases in intensity until the noise is almost deafening. Nance sits up, looks out at the rain, then puts his head down again.

My eyelids start to droop, and I find a place under the centre of the awning where the raindrops cannot reach me and lie down. At least the wind has stopped. Again I think of my wife and the kids and wonder if they miss me.

I am the first to waken. When the rain stopped I don't know, but the sky is still covered with clouds. Behind us, to the east, I can see a faint glow on the horizon. Then, almost as if by magic, the clouds disperse and the sun, rising over the trees, bathes the river and forest in crimson light. The Malay unfolds his blanket and stands. We peer up and down the river but can see no sign of the canoes or the escort. I shrug and try to show by gestures that I do not understand what has happened to them, but that we should wait for a while before we continue moving. The Malay goes to the stove and tries to light it. This poses a problem, because the rain has soaked everything.

Nance is up now. He nods to me and goes to the end of the boat and urinates into the river. The sound of piss hitting the water seems strangely loud in the stillness of the morning. When he finishes he fishes a bucket of water out of the stream and splashes it over himself and then wipes himself dry. He is the only one of us who is still doing this. I can smell Montgomery at a distance of six feet and Johnson stunk even before the trip upriver began. I have never seen the Malay bathe but he does not smell at all. I know that even under ordinary conditions the body odour of westerners is offensive to orientals, and I wonder what his thoughts about us are now –

probably he thinks we are a bunch of pigs. I bend over the side of the boat and look at the reflection of my face in the river. My hair is dishevelled and a week's growth of stubble covers my chin. There is shaving soap and a razor in my gear, but I haven't thought to shave even though I've had plenty of time to do so. I'm a meticulous person. My slovenliness amazes me, and I ascribe it to the jungle and anxiety over the Japs. This mission is getting to me – there is no doubt about that.

The Malay has finally managed to light a fire in his stove and is brewing some coffee. He takes down his fishing pole, points to the river, and hands it to Nance. Nance indicates that there is no bait for the hooks and the Malay reaches down into the water and holds his arm there for a moment. When he lifts it up it is covered with leeches. He lights a cigarette and burns them off, taking care so that only the heads sizzle. Now Nance has his bait.

Inside of fifteen minutes Nance has caught a dozen fish. Some are fat, silver-grey fish like those he caught lower down on the Kayan; others are slender and eel-like with sharp teeth. When he pulls these fish out of the water their sides contain almost a complete rainbow of colours, but as soon as he thumps them against the deck, breaking their backbone, they turn a dull green. The Malay takes the fish and guts and scales them with the long, curved knife he carries in his belt; then he flips them into two large frying pans that he has put on the stove. He takes one from a pile of coconuts he has brought along, opens it with a machete, and pours the milk into the skillet. It splatters and smokes, but the smell of the coconut mixed with the smell of frying fish is delicious.

Now that all of the work is done Johnson and Montgomery climb out from under the awning. If I look bad they look worse. Johnson is gaunt and there are dark circles under his eyes; Montgomery has a wild look in his eyes that is frightening and he still clutches his rifle.

The Malay hands out the fish on greasy tin plates, but it is sizzling hot and we are so hungry that we don't care about the plates. We have to eat with our fingers and the hot fish burns us, but nobody complains; then we drink coffee.

Johnson belches and picks his teeth. Montgomery goes to a place near the bow and sits down, resting his chin on his knees, and peers gloomily downriver in the direction we have come from. I am worried about him but there is nothing I can do. Before we started up the river he seemed the strongest among us, the one least likely to crack. He has a Medal of Honor and a Purple Heart and was once written up in *Stars and Stripes*. Now he's close to lunacy. It must be the jungle, it has to be, but I don't understand how or why. It's God-awful hot but it's not the heat alone – and Montgomery has fought Japs before. Johnson is a wreck too but he'll probably survive. I don't think Montgomery will. Something tells me right now that he's a dead man.

Suddenly the warriors appear, sliding their canoes out of the trees and down the river-bank directly opposite us. The V is formed again and a man in the lead canoe points upstream, and the Malay starts the motor. It coughs a few times before turning over; then we are on our way again. If the men in the canoes are worn by the battle or the rowing, they do not show it. If anything, they seem to be stronger than the day before, and the canoes raise small wakes as they plow through the glass-smooth water.

Nance asks me where we are, and I show him the Dutchman's map. I point to where I think we are but he shakes his head.

'Here's the fork, Captain,' he says. 'This was the place where the other war party attacked – this straight stretch here. We're just about here now.'

He's right and I nod. According to the map we are in the Iran Mountains. The river passes completely through them and connects with a tributary of the Rajang. The Rajang drains into the South China Sea on Borneo's north-west coast, and if the river were navigable the whole way we could use it to cross the entire island, but it isn't. Midway in the mountains are three sets of diagonal lines that indicate more rapids, and printed beside them are the words 'niet bevaarbar'. The river twists and turns in the mountains, following valleys that are arranged haphazardly, as if they had been created by some malicious force. According to the intelligence briefing I received, it is impossible even for the natives to travel on foot in these mountains. They are too rugged and too heavily forested. The rivers are the only link with the outside. Why a man – any man – would willingly seek out such a place is a mystery, but the man we are going to meet has been living in these mountains for nearly ten years.

Towards mid-afternoon I notice a change in the river. The current has speeded up again, so much so that the rocks near the shore are covered with foam. The Malay has the motor open full-throttle but still our speed has slowed considerably. Even the rowers in the canoes seem affected and are labouring. I look at the map again and see a place marked 'waterval'. It is difficult to tell how close we are to it, but if there is a falls near that would explain the power of the current here.

The river squeezes between two large bluffs. Vines hang from their sides, trailing into the water. There are monkeys in these vines and we can hear them chattering high overhead. The passage is so narrow that it is almost like a cave, and for a few moments the sunlight is completely blocked; then the river opens out into a small lake, lying in a cup formed by four tree-covered mountains. The lake is perhaps half a mile in diameter and the steep, tree-covered sides of the mountains drop down almost perpendicular to its edge. At the far end there is a waterfall, the water plunging from a great height down the side of one of the mountains and into the lake where it raises a cloud of mist. We peer up the mountainside, trying to see the source of the waterfall, but half a mile up everything is shrouded in low-hanging clouds. The air is cool and I shiver.

The canoes are resting in the middle of the lake, bobbing up and down in the rough water. A man in one of them stands and makes a sound like the owlish hoot we heard in the night. The roar of the falls is deafening, but the sound echoes clear and distinct. From far above on the tree-covered side of the mountain comes an answering hoot. The canoes move towards the falls and we watch in amazement as, one after the other, they pass through the falling water and disappear from sight. Finally a man in the last canoe beckons to us.

The Malay is nervous, but I point after the canoes and he follows them. The surface of the lake in front of the bottom of the falls is very rough, and we rock wildly in the swells; then we are in the falling water and can see nothing. We pass through it in a few seconds and find ourselves in total darkness, floating in a cavern inside the rocky mountain side. In a few moments our eyes adjust and we can see light coming from a place to our right. The Malay steers the boat in this direction and we float up to a crude stone pier, at the end of which is a large hole where the light enters the cavern. The canoes are already tied to the pier and some of the warriors are standing there, the white paint on their faces making them look like ghosts in the darkness.

We unload our gear and climb out. Each man except the Malay carries a backpack. We all bring handguns and rifles.

When we emerge from the cave we find ourselves on the side of the mountain on a path leading directly under the falls. The cascading water screens this place, so that from the surface of the lake it cannot be seen. The path leads upward, weaving sharply back and forth as it climbs the hillside. When it is several hundred feet above the lake, it turns into the thick forest that covers the mountainside. Here the path is less tortuous, but we continue to zig and zag our way up the mountain. From time to time we catch glimpses of the lake through gaps in the trees; then we enter the clouds, a thick mist fills the air and everything is dripping wet.

For almost an hour we climb; then the path levels out as we pass over the crown of the mountains.

Suddenly there is a dazzling light and we are standing in a clearing overlooking a wide valley. The floor of the valley is covered with rice paddies which extend, in terraces, part way up both of its sides. The path enters the forest again and we descend until we reach the floor of the valley. Here we rest for a while.

Men are working in the paddies. They have wide, flat hats and are naked except for a strip of cloth wrapped around their loins. They look at us but do not seem especially surprised or interested and continue their work. We follow a path that leads between rice paddies for two or three miles then start to climb up the near side of the valley. Halfway up, gleaming in the sunshine, is a large building shaped like a great warehouse and standing on stilts. One of the warriors points to it, saying, 'rumah.' As we approach the building, several children run to greet us. They are naked but look well-fed and, showing dazzling white teeth, they smile at us. Bare-breasted, graceful women with brightly-coloured sarongs wrapped about their hips pass us, carrying water jugs and baskets of laundry on their heads. They smile coquettishly and one of them stares at Nance. More children appear: these are boys, older than the first ones we saw – about half a dozen of them, ten or eleven years of age. They watch us and then talk rapidly to each other. One of the men in the escort party speaks to them and then they dash ahead up the hill towards the large building.

Finally we reach the base of the building and climb up a log that has steps carved into it. The supporting stilts are about thirty feet high, and when we reach the top of the log there is a floor made of bamboo, covered with palm leaves and ferns. This is an open space, a sort of porch, and it is filled with people, most of whom stop what they are doing to stare at us.

One of the escorts says something to the Malay, and he turns to me and says, 'We must wait here.'

I peer off over the valley. It seems to go on for miles, and everywhere – the floor, the sides – is covered with rice paddies. The sun is bright, but clouds are racing overhead so that some of the valley is bathed in dazzling light while other parts lie in shadow. I hear voices and look towards the entrance of the building. It is high and arched and a fringe of vines or leather thongs hangs down from the top of the arch. What appear to be coconuts are tied to the ends of several of these thongs, but when I look more closely I see that these are not coconuts – they have eyes and noses and lips.

A crowd of people is standing in the doorway, in the middle is a slender, light-skinned man with aristocratic features. The man of God has come to meet us.

IV

He gives me a peculiar feeling when he speaks. At first I don't
understand why this is, but then it dawns on me. The priest is
speaking to me but his eyes are not meeting mine. Not that he
is avoiding my eyes – or if he is he hides this – but rather that,
although he is looking at me, he sees something else. His eyes
seem to be focused on something behind me, and when he
regards me it is as if I am merely a detail in the foreground of a
large picture. And there is something about his voice that is
unsettling. He speaks American English, yet he does not look
American – French perhaps or Italian. Even his speech is
strange; it's cultivated and correct, almost pedantic, yet there's
a trace of something else in it that I can't quite figure out. It
might be Brooklynese but I can't be sure.

'Your journey was difficult?' he asks.

It is the expected question to which I give the expected
answer.

'And your health and the health of your crew?'

My eyes go to Montgomery and Johnson, who are standing
about ten feet from us, gaping at the village women. They look
like two skid row derelicts.

'Some of my men found the trip difficult,' I say.

'You can rest here and regain your strength. We have ade-
quate food and the place is peaceful.'

I remember the heads hanging from the arch he has just
passed under.

He asks me what I do at home when I am not playing soldier.
I tell him.

32

'I knew you were not a career soldier,' he says. 'Your face is filled with thought. Professional soldiers do not look like this.'

I ask him what professional soldiers look like and he gives me a strange, knowing smile.

'Professional soldiers look many ways, but they usually do not have faces like yours. A teacher must read many books, and to read many books and be a soldier are not . . . how shall I say?' – he fishes for a word and I watch his face work; it is a strange face, filled with a curious luminescence. There is something attractive but at the same time unsettling about him. 'Compatible – that's the word I seek. A soldier must act. He must not think too much for too much thought paralyses the will.'

I tell him that a paralysed will has always been one of my problems, and he smiles indulgently.

For a while longer we make small-talk; then he rises.

'I must go,' he says. 'You will be shown to rooms and given food. You should try to rest and regain your strength. Do not worry – you can trust these people. As long as you do nothing to harm them they will leave you in peace.'

Again my eyes move to the heads hanging from the arch, but if he notices he says nothing.

The building which keeps the sun and rain from our heads is like a great, open-ended warehouse. The roof is peaked and at its highest point is almost forty feet above the platform that rests on stilts. The platform itself is bamboo, but on top of the bamboo base is a rough rug of ferns and palm fronds. A large hallway runs down the centre of the building, and this is filled with people coming and going, with playing children and gossiping old women. We are each given a room, which is really a space screened off by walls also made of woven palm fronds. A row of these spaces is ranged on both sides of the central hallway. Some are large – holding entire families – but most are about ten by fifteen. Inside these is a pallet to sleep on but otherwise the room is bare. At the entrance there is a curtain made of palm leaves, screening off the room from the central hallway. There is a hole in the centre of the floor about two feet in diameter. The floor around it is stained red by the juice of betel nuts which the natives chew. I assume the hole serves as a sort of spittoon.

A woman appears, carrying bowls of coconut milk, roasted yams and rice cakes. We are very hungry, and the food tastes delicious. Our rooms are in a row so we can talk to each other without leaving them, but we are all very tired and soon sleep.

When I waken, several hours have passed. Night has come and the hallway is lit by torches. I can hear much coming and going outside my room, and shortly the woman appears again, carrying a tray with food on it. This time there is roast meat of some sort that tastes like pork and rice and fruit. There is also more fermented coconut milk to drink.

After I have finished eating I leave my room and stroll down the hallway. The building is a beehive of activity; some of the people are eating, squatting in groups around clay pots of meat and rice. None of the rooms have fires in them – the building would probably burn like tinder – but there is a great fire in a clearing just beyond the house; here water is boiled along with half a dozen other things in various pots hanging on a chain stretched between two stakes. Old women tend the fire, and children, mostly young boys, bring wood to keep it burning. In this place that probably constitutes a real task, for almost all the wood in the forest is too wet to burn well. Where the boys find dry wood is a mystery. Even here, in the uplands, the air is humid, but it is much more comfortable than it was lower down, for the evenings at least are cool.

After the people have eaten, the sound of voices gradually begins to die down. For a while, women hurry to and fro, carrying pots back and forth or bringing water to their rooms. When I peer into the cubicles, I can see that already the children are sleeping. Nance joins me, and we stroll up and down the corridor together.

'It's like home, Captain,' he says. 'This place reminds me of the building I used to live in in Newark. Come summer and everybody had to leave their door open 'cause it got so hot.'

I watch his eyes follow a woman who passes, carrying a sleeping child on her back.

'I can't figure this place,' he says. 'We all know what those things are hanging back there' – he gestures towards the archway where the heads hang, like so many pieces of fruit – 'but these people ain't mean – you can see that.'

'You've only been here half a day,' I say. 'You can't be certain about anything yet.'

He shakes his head. 'No, Captain – I don't think you're right there. I can tell meanness when I see it. When you grow up where I grew up you learn to do that – you gotta if you want to stay alive. These people ain't mean, Captain.'

The hallway is empty except for the two of us, and it is very quiet. From a few rooms we can hear snoring or voices talking softly; otherwise there is total silence. We go to the end of the hall and pass under the heads, stopping for a moment to look up at them. The faces are shrunken into grotesque scowls, but the features are still discernible. The faces are like those of the men who attacked the escort party. On some of them we can still see the white paint that the warriors wore.

We go outside and stand on the porch and study the sky. Clouds cover the moon. We can hear the buzz of mosquitoes, but most of them seem to be beyond the porch, close to the ground. Up here a soft but steady breeze is blowing with just enough force to make it impossible for the mosquitoes to hover. If we were on the ground we would be eaten alive, but on the porch they do not bother us.

The clouds covering the moon make the night very dark. There is a faint glimmer where some rice paddies lie, but otherwise, total blackness. Yet the sinister feeling that surrounded us below, in the jungle, does not exist here. The night sounds are different; instead of the unnerving cries of the hunting and the hunted, we hear only the soft woosh of the wind. I take out a pack of cigarettes and offer one to Nance. We smoke in silence for a while then become aware that someone else has come out on to the porch. It is a woman, but otherwise we can tell nothing because it is so dark. She is standing about fifteen feet from us. Her presence seems to unsettle Nance. When he has smoked the cigarette down to a stub he hurls the glowing butt out into the darkness, shooting a quick glance in the woman's direction as he does so. It's been a long time since either of us has been with a woman, and I can imagine what he's feeling.

'How long we goin' to be in this place, Captain?' he asks.

'I don't know,' I say. 'It depends on the priest.'

'Something strange about that man,' he says. 'My grandmother used to call people like that anointed ones. They always give me the creeps. They ain't like regular people – you can't ever tell what's on their mind.'

Somewhere beyond us two birds fly through the night air, cawing softly as they go. The wind seems to stop for a minute, and then suddenly the rain comes. It is hard, heavy rain and we make for the archway quickly; then, once inside, turn to stare back into the darkness.

The woman has joined us and now stands just opposite. Her sarong is soaked and clings to her, revealing small, high breasts and gently swelling hips. Her hair is piled on top of her head, twisted into a knot and secured with an ivory pin. She is watching us intently, the way a curious child might. I take out a cigarette and light it. Nance reaches for his pack then fumbles and it falls to the floor. As he stoops to pick it up, the woman's eyes follow his movements.

'Why don't you give her a cigarette?' I ask, and he looks at me as if I'm crazy.

'Go ahead,' I say, and he tamps the pack so one cigarette stands up then holds the pack out to the woman. She looks confused, and I tell him to hand the cigarette to her. She takes it from him, inspects it, then puts it carefully between her lips.

'Give her a light,' I say, and he does so, cupping his hands to shield the flickering flame from the wind. The girl puffs on the cigarette, raising a great cloud of smoke. After a minute she looks towards Nance and smiles. She cannot be older than sixteen or seventeen, but there is something very knowing in that smile.

'I think she's the local talent,' I say.

The girl stares at Nance, and I can tell she is making him nervous.

I finish my cigarette and flick it out into the driving rain then say 'good-night' and start to leave. An expression of panic crosses Nance's face, and I wink at him.

Just before I push the curtain to my room aside to enter, I turn and look up the hallway. The girl and Nance are still standing just inside the archway, but she has moved closer to him, inspecting something that he has given her. I cannot be certain at this distance, but it looks like it's his dog tag.

The sound of laughing children wakens me. I rise, stretch, and walk to the doorway and push back the curtain. Morning light fills the hallway, and directly across from me the curtain is pushed back from the entranceway of a large room where two small children stand, staring at me. I raise my hands and make claws out of them and growl at the children. For a minute they

36

look frightened; then one of them – the boy – begins to giggle, and soon the girl joins in. I stick my tongue out at them and they stick their tongues out at me. I ruffle my hair and make menacing movements with my hands, and they squeal and hide behind two large wooden pillars that stand on each side of the entranceway to their room. From behind these, they peek out cautiously; then, when they see me, squeal again.

An old woman passing in the hallway with a large jug on her head looks towards me, sees the wild expression on my face and my hands raised like claws, and rushes away in terror.

The curtain in front of the room to my right is pushed back, and Montgomery steps out and stretches. He looks towards me and I notice that the paranoid gleam is still in his eyes. Then Johnson's head appears in the next doorway. He has a long, scrawny neck, and when he pushes his head out of the doorway and twists towards me he looks like a vulture. I ask how he slept and he says, 'lousy.'

Nance appears in the doorway of the room to my left with a sheepish expression on his face. I don't know what time it was when he returned to his room, but I do know that the sun had already risen, because the outer wall of my room was glowing in the early morning light.

Nance stretches and goes down the hallway and outside. There is a jauntiness to his step that he didn't have yesterday. I follow him. Once outside, we climb down the ladder and walk along a pathway that leads between two rice paddies to a place where a splashing stream comes down from high on the ridge of the mountain. There is a small waterfall here and below it a pool of water in which a dozen kids are swimming around like fish.

The water is surprisingly cold. We splash it on our faces and necks then plunge into the pool and paddle around in our briefs.

After a few minutes we scramble out of the pool and stand in the sunshine to dry ourselves. Twenty yards below the pool a path leads up to the stream that drains it; there is a bridge of stones in this stream, and then the path continues to another stream about a hundred yards away. Here there is an almost identical waterfall and pool.

Several women descend from the porch and march along this path. They cross over the bridge made of wading stones, looking at us as they do. One of them whispers something into the ear of the woman immediately in front of her, and they both giggle.

We watch them cross to the other pool, then crouch down to wash their long hair in the water; finally, they unwrap their sarongs and slide quietly into the water.

When we are dry we pull our clothes back on and go back to the long house. A few minutes after we reach our rooms the woman arrives, carrying trays of fruit and rice cakes and a hot liquid that tastes almost like tea. We eat, each in his room sitting cross-legged on the floor. I can hear Johnson and Montgomery talking. Their voices are low, so that I have difficulty making out the words, but I can understand snatches of what they are saying. Montgomery is complaining and Johnson is egging him on. He doesn't trust the 'niggers' in this place, and he doesn't much like the 'nigger' who's on the mission with them. The captain is one of those smart-assed college boys who knows it all. From Johnson I would expect this, but to hear it coming from Montgomery is a shock. He's near the breaking point already, and I don't think it will take much more to push him over the edge.

After I finish eating I stretch out and smoke. It feels good to be off the river and not to have to worry about being shot by a Jap or a Dayak using a blowgun. This place is pleasant enough and it intrigues me. There are lots of ways to fight a war, and right now this way seems better than most. Instead of lying back and smoking, I might be in a landing craft, trying to storm a fortified beach defended by a bunch of Jap soldiers pledged to die rather than yield; or I might be trying to fight my way through Italy, with an enemy soldier hiding in every ditch, ready to blow my head off.

There is a soft tap at the entrance and I sit up. Whoever is outside says something that I can't understand, so I stand and push the curtain aside. The priest is there.

'I trust you have slept well,' he says, and we both sit. 'And the food? . . . have you had your breakfast?'

I tell him that we have eaten and that the food was good. That seems to please him.

'So you see this place has a hospitable side to it – it is not as bad as some people say.'

'You have been here alone for a long time,' I reply. 'It must get lonely sometimes. You must miss your family and friends.'

He shakes his head, 'No – I have lived here so long that it has become my home. Five from my class were sent to Borneo, but only I stayed. The others all left after a year; some stayed only a few months. They found the life too hard, but I would feel uncomfortable anywhere else.'

'But now the Japanese know of you,' I say. 'They are sending men to take you captive.'

He looks at me then shakes his head again.

'They will never come here. They stay on the coast near Tarakan and Beaufort where there is oil. They will not come this far inland.'

'You are wrong,' I say. 'Already a large column has been sent from Tarakan. They will not reach you for several days – probably not for weeks. But they will come.'

'I do not believe that,' he says. 'And even if they would come here they could not make me go. I have been in this place too long.'

'The Japanese are fighting a war,' I say. 'They care only about winning, and to them you are an enemy agent.'

He looks unsettled and abruptly stands.

'I must go now,' he says. 'We can talk of these things at another time.'

Before I can reply he has gone.

In the afternoon I stay inside. The sun is hot, and the people take their afternoon meal then sleep. It is very quiet. Nance comes to visit me and asks about my conversation with the priest. 'He's a little less than eager to go,' I tell him.

After Nance has left, I get up and walk in the hallway for a while. It is hot here; the breeze that blew throughout the night has died, but as long as I am shielded from the naked glare of the sun, the heat is at least tolerable.

I have reached the far end of the hallway when I hear a rustle, and the curtain before a doorway is pushed back and a young woman steps out. She is breathtakingly beautiful, with large, almond-shaped eyes and a heart-shaped face with prominent cheekbones. When she sees me a worried look appears on her face, and she hurries past me with averted eyes. I continue to the end of the passageway, turn, and start back towards the other end. When I reach it, I stand under the archway and look out. The midday sunlight is dazzling, and the water in the rice paddies glitters. Except for a few puffy clouds to the east, the sky is clear.

After about ten minutes I turn to go back to my room. I see the priest emerge from a room at the other end of the hallway. He has a distracted look, as if he is absorbed in thought. It is only later, when I am in my room again, lying on my back staring at the patterns which the sunlight makes on the bamboo wall, that I realize that the priest came out of the same room as the beautiful woman.

V

'We can't wait forever. If the Nips catch us here they'll cut our balls off.'

Johnson is talking to me – he's been talking for fifteen minutes, and everything he has said adds up to the same thing: He wants to leave now. Montgomery is standing beside him. Montgomery hasn't said much; he just hovers in the background, holding his rifle and looking at me with a stare that belongs in Bedlam.

'We've been here one night and a day,' I say, 'not even that. The Japs are still a long way away. You saw that jungle. They'll be lucky if they can cut their way through it in a month – and then they have to find the path behind the waterfall. We've got lots of time.'

Johnson isn't convinced. Something has put a bug up his ass, but I don't know what. I don't think he wanted to come on this mission in the first place. I tell him this, and he looks surprised then gives me a cunning smile, the kind of smile that says, 'You caught me, pal – now let's see what you're gonna do about it.'

'We wait here until the priest decides to come,' I say. 'We were sent here to get him and we don't leave without him. It's as simple as that, and you better get it through your head.'

He curses and throws the curtain out of the way as he leaves. Montgomery stays, continuing to stare at me with half-mad eyes.

'You're a soldier,' I say. 'You know what orders are. I'm following them. That's how I play this game.'

'This place isn't right, Captain,' he says, glancing over his shoulder as if he's afraid someone will hear him. 'The people in

41

this place aren't civilized. You can't trust them. I'd rather take my chances out there in the jungle with the Japs.'

'They haven't bothered us yet,' I say. 'In fact, if it wasn't for the Kelabit we probably would never have made it this far.'

'Yeah,' he says. 'That's just what I'm thinking. They helped us come here, didn't they? They wanted us here. That don't seem right to me. I'm thinking they got a reason.' I want to tell him he thinks too much but don't. 'There's something wrong with that priest too – there's something weird about that guy. He's been here too long. How do we know he isn't working with the Japs? How do we know he isn't trying to set us up?'

The glitter in his eyes seems brighter now, and he is gripping his rifle so tightly that the knuckles on his hand have turned bone-white.

'You've got to keep cool, Montgomery,' I say. 'You're letting your feelings get the upper hand. You know how things are. We came to take the priest out, and when we go he comes with us – and if that means we wait for a week until he makes up his mind, then we wait.'

Now he is staring at me with a different kind of look – one that says I'm his enemy. I can see his trigger finger moving up and down nervously.

'You're getting too upset, Montgomery,' I say. 'Everything is going to be all right. We're going to get out of here all right. Just try and take it easy for a while. Get some sleep. You look like a wreck.'

His eyes narrow but he says nothing. For an entire minute we stare at each other, and a little voice in the back of my head keeps saying, 'This is it – the crazy bastard is going to shoot you!'

Then he wheels, pushes the curtain out of the way and is gone. My hands are trembling, and I can feel the sweat running down my back.

After Montgomery leaves I go out to the porch and smoke. It's a grey day and a thick mist fills the air, so that it is difficult to see the tops of the hills. Last night the rain fell; it has stopped now, but everything is dripping wet. Most of the Kelabit are inside their long house, but I can see a small group of men squatting in a circle near the fire that is used to boil water. They have rigged up a spit and are turning it slowly, roasting a joint of meat over the glowing coals. It's odd that they should be outside in this weather, and it is not the right time of day to be preparing a meal.

As I watch, they tear off a large chunk of meat and pass it around the circle, each taking a bite then passing it on to the next man. They repeat this three times; then one of the men lifts up something from the ground and begins to swing it back and forth. It takes a few moments before it registers on me that this object is a head, and that the man is swinging it by the hair. Abruptly the men rise and walk off single-file up the hill, where they disappear into the mist. Two of them carry the spit, resting the long pole, laden with meat, across their shoulders.

For a long time I do not move, then I toss the glowing stub of my cigarette away and light another. The rain begins again, but it is soft, hardly more than mist. Two women carrying large clay jugs appear under the arch; they cross the porch, descend the log that functions as a stairway, and walk to the fire where they tilt the great water pot and fill their jugs. When they return, their faces and hair are beaded with raindrops.

The rain stops then starts again. I am soaked, but the air is warm and the wetness refreshing. The mist has thickened and now extends farther down the mountain to a place not thirty yards above the long house. Suddenly, from out of it, appears a lone man, then another and another. They march steadily towards the long house, moving with slow, almost somnambulistic steps. When they reach the log stairway, they mount it and pass by me, still single file. Their eyes are glassy and they stare straight ahead. I recognize them now – they are the same men who marched off carrying the meat-laden spit. As they pass by me it seems as if they are in a trance. None of them takes the slightest notice of me, and I turn to watch them vanish under the arch decorated with heads. Hanging from the belt of the last man is a fresh head.

'I saw it, Captain, so did Johnson and Montgomery. It's spooked Montgomery. He's talking crazy, Captain.'

Nance is standing in my room. It's early evening. The fog has thickened, and the air outside the long house is now almost liquid. The temperature has not fallen, however; if anything, the warmth has increased, so that now it is suffocatingly heavy. I can see the perspiration dripping off Nance's nose and chin. He is wearing only his briefs.

'There was a noise in the hallway, Captain. I went out. They were passing, a whole row of them, and the last guy had a head hanging from his belt. It was fresh, Captain – the blood was still dripping from the neck. Those dudes must have been taking some drug, 'cause they looked like zombies. Johnson heard the noise too, 'cause next thing I noticed his head was sticking out of the doorway of his room. Then he called Montgomery, and he saw it too.'

'Johnson *called* Montgomery?'

Nance nods. 'It didn't seem to affect Johnson much, but Montgomery went bananas. I heard him talking – half to himself, half for Johnson's sake. He's been doing that a lot lately so I don't pay much attention to him, but this time it was different. The man thinks that the people here will come after him next.'

'Montgomery's gone around the bend,' I say. 'The only thing we can do for him is to try and make sure he doesn't get into trouble. We better keep Johnson away from him.'

Nance looks worried.

'They only hunt their enemies, Nance – didn't you read the briefing? It's part of their religion. As long as we are staying with them – as long as we're inside this long house – we're safe.'

Nance says he understands, but he doesn't look very comfortable.

An hour passes. The air is the same – so humid that it feels like I should be swimming in it instead of trying to breathe it. I rise and go down the hallway and out on to the porch again. The fog is even thicker, but now people are moving about in it, women coming and going from the fire, children playing games. They look as if they are walking on fields of grey cotton.

Two people come out from under the archway and stand for a moment, talking in low voices. Then they climb down the log stairway and begin to cross the open space before the fire. One of them is the priest, the other is the beautiful woman with the large eyes. When they reach a group of men standing near the fire, they speak for a few minutes then turn and walk off up the mountainside where they vanish into the fog.

I wait a little while then go back inside the building. It's time to check on Montgomery. I've been putting this off, but I can't avoid it forever.

Outside his room I hesitate and call his name. There is no

answer, so I push the curtain back: the room is empty and completely bare – his knapsack and rifle are gone. This can mean only one thing. Quickly I rush to Nance's room, and then we hurry outside and stand helplessly on the porch, peering into the fog. Montgomery is somewhere out there. Whether he's heading north across the mountains or south-west along the river we don't know, but for all practical purposes it doesn't make much difference. He might as well be on the moon.

VI

'Your friend has done a very regrettable thing,' says the priest. 'The jungle is not a place for a man who does not know this country. Even the men in this long house are fearful of going alone into it. There are no paths, no trails.'

'Is there any hope of finding him?' I ask and he shrugs. 'Perhaps a hunter could find his trail,' I say.

'I will talk with the men, but what you ask is almost impossible, and even if it were possible the men would not want to go.'

'But you have influence with them,' I say. 'Surely you could persuade them.'

'This is only one tribe,' he says. 'There are other tribes in this region, and they are not friendly. The men do not like to leave their own land. To do so is dangerous. In certain seasons it is reasonably safe but not now.'

I ask why.

'It is planting season,' he says. 'The tribes look for' – he pauses, as if he does not want to go farther. 'They look for victims for sacrifice. They believe that for their soil to be fertile – for their rice to grow and flourish – the spirits of many men are needed. They think this spirit resides inside each man and can be released only with his death.'

'And so they take heads,' I say. He nods.

'The people call it touching meat. Until a man has done it he is not considered a man – no woman will have him as husband.'

'And the flesh?' I ask. 'The body?'

'It is eaten,' he says.

Sunlight filters down through the leaves. We are making our way through dense, almost impenetrable, jungle. At the head of the column is a man wielding a great knife like a machete. We have been cutting our way through the jungle for hours, following a trail that the best tracker in the long house thinks is Montgomery's. I am not certain. The only indication that a living creature has passed this way is an occasional bent twig or twisted leaf. Perhaps it was Montgomery who did this, but to me it seems just as likely that it was a deer or a wild pig.

According to my calculations we have only three or, at most, four hours of light left. Before the light dies we will have to turn back, for none of the natives wants to spend the night in the jungle. It's hopeless; trying to find a lone man in the rain forest of eastern Borneo is like looking for a needle in a haystack, the difference being that this haystack is filled with a million stinging insects and poisonous snakes. Already I have been bitten so many times that my face feels like a pincushion.

There are twenty men with me – young warriors who have chosen to follow me into the jungle to prove their manhood. We have been travelling for almost ten hours, hacking our way through the jungle covering the foothills of the Iran Mountains. Our progress has been slow, but it cannot have been slower than Montgomery's, for these men know the mountains and the jungle.

We move two abreast with warriors at the front and back of the column carrying strung bows and drawn knives. The Kelabit look tense. They have not painted their faces with the white paint of a war party, but they are prepared to fight. Before we left the long house the men in the party made a sort of prayer, and each took a small bag of brown leaves with him. Every few miles they take one of these leaves out and chew it. Nance asks for one, and when he has chewed it for a few minutes he looks towards me and smiles.

'This stuff floats you Captain. These guys could probably go for days on what they have in each one of those little pouches.'

He may be right but we'll never know for sure, because soon night will fall and by then we'll be back in the long house. The Kelabit believe that evil spirits roam in the darkness, hunting for bodies to enter. These spirits are supposed to enter through a man's nostrils and ears and take possession of his soul. When that happens he either goes mad or dies. The priest has told me all of this, and while he spoke his eyes moved quickly from side to side, like those of a man looking for something – something which he fears seeing. It is almost as if he believes in these spirits too.

We reach the top of a ridge and the warriors stop. One man points off towards the distant peaks of the Iran Mountains. These are forested almost to the summit, but nonetheless they are imposing. The man points first towards the mountains then towards the sun, which is now not far above the western horizon. He tries to tell me something but I don't understand; then he takes two hands and holds his neck and makes a croaking sound. The gesture is universal, but still I pretend I do not understand. Finally, in exasperation, he motions impatiently that we should return in the direction of the long house. The others in the party are already nervous, their eyes fixed on the fast-sinking ball of red fire which is not far above the western horizon. Even if we make very good time we will not reach the long house before nightfall. The men know this and they are afraid.

Scarcely half the distance back to the long house has been covered when the thickening shadows give way to total darkness. The sensation is eerie. Sounds that earlier in the day were insignificant – the cry of a monkey, the soft chirping of insects – become ominous. The pale moonlight does not penetrate through the foliage and we must move blindly. Leaves and vines wipe our faces; roots reach out to trip us. The air is filled with insects of all sorts; they get in our eyes and nostrils. Several times we hear a large animal moving in the undergrowth not more than fifteen or twenty feet from us. It could be a leopard or a wild boar. Or, worse still, men from another tribe tracking us, seeking heads.

I cannot see the faces of the warriors, but I can sense their mounting panic. Then I hear it: a strange, indescribably eerie cry, half human, half animal. The men stop as if frozen. They whisper to each other. Then suddenly begin to move again. Now we are going much faster, halfway between a brisk trot and a flat-out run. Branches slap us in the face. We stumble over roots, fall, scramble to our feet and plunge ahead again. Our lungs are burning. But we are unable to escape from the weird cry. It follows us, rising sometimes to a hysterical wail then sinking to a soft, sobbing moan. A man falls directly in front of me, and I stumble over him and go down. The sound grows nearer. I cover my ears with my hands and peer wildly around. There is nothing but blackness, total, as dark as death itself. A cold chill goes through me and I begin to shiver violently; then it is quiet.

But the silence is even worse. A great dread sweeps through me, and suddenly I hear a wild, hysterical shriek. It grows louder and louder. Something grabs my shoulder and begins to shake me violently. I swing my fist blindly and strike something hard. I am thrown down, and it is on me. We grapple, rolling over and over.

I see Nance's face, bleeding at the mouth, his forehead covered with beads of sweat.

'Take it easy!' he says. 'You nearly killed me!'

'Did you hear it?' I ask, gasping for breath. 'You had to hear it – that crazy moan and then the shriek.'

The sound has gone now, and in its place are the usual night sounds of the jungle, the cries of monkeys and the hum of insects. Yet only a few minutes ago I heard the sound. Or did I? Was it all my imagination? Has the jungle finally gotten to me? I need to know.

'Didn't you hear it too, Nance?' I ask, half fearful that he will give the wrong answer.

'I heard it, Cap,' he says and I relax.

'What could it have been? The wind? It must have been the wind.'

'No wind sounds like that, Cap – that wasn't the wind.'

We start walking again, making our way in the direction in which we think the long house lies. The darkness is still overwhelming, but the moon has grown brighter, and now we can sometimes see it through holes in the roof of the forest. Now it is only Nance and me. The men who were with us have fled. They know the way back to the long house better than we do, so we assume they are already there, safe, shaking with fear and telling whoever will listen about the spirits that attacked them. Both of us are still shaken, but I am by far the more upset. I can still hear the strange moan and feel the icy coldness that seemed to go through me. Over and over again, I tell myself that it was all foolishness – that there are no spirits – but part of me now believes otherwise.

For an hour we walk then stop to rest. We are both perspiring heavily, and the mosquitoes have become ravenous. If we do not continually move our hands before our faces they bite us on the eyelids and lips. Already our faces and the exposed parts of our bodies – our necks and wrists and hands – are numb. And we are tired. We cannot go more than fifty feet without stumbling over the root of a tree or one of the vines that stretch, like a vast cobweb, throughout the forest.

Suddenly Nance grabs my arm and pulls me to the ground, at the same time putting a finger to his lips. We crawl to a thick tree trunk and crouch behind it. A minute passes then another. The mosquitoes are worse close to the ground and are driving me crazy. I start to stand but Nance holds me down.

Then I hear what he heard. Somewhere nearby – the distance cannot be more than twenty-five yards – something or someone is moving through the forest. We can hear twigs snapping and the rustle of leaves. The sound stops and we hold our breath; then it starts again. Now it seems to be moving more slowly, almost cautiously, as if whatever is out there senses our presence. We draw our pistols and wait. The sound is more distinct now. Whatever kind of creature it is, it is stepping very lightly, for we cannot hear individual footsteps.

There is a chirping sound and a dozen bats flit through the forest, up high, just below the umbrella of foliage at the top of the trees. They circle then return, this time flying much lower. Somewhere near us they land. The forest is full of fruit, and they are probably feeding on it. Slowly Nance stands and begins to move off, motioning that I should follow him. I have taken a half dozen steps when Nance screams. Then there is the sound of vegetation being torn, as if a fierce struggle is taking place. I rush forward into the darkness and trip over Nance. He is writhing on the ground and wrapped around him, like a great steel spring, is a python as thick as my thigh. The snake's head is lashing back and forth, but the trunk is steady, contracting like a powerful vise. Already Nance is gasping for breath. I cannot shoot the snake without hitting Nance, and my efforts to pry it loose have no effect.

I grab my knife and try to cut through it. The skin is as tough as leather. I saw back and forth and my hands are sticky with blood, but the coils continue to tighten.

'The head!' croaks Nance. 'Go for the head!'

I can't see it in the darkness, so I must work my hands up the long trunk a foot at a time, until I feel the trunk grow thinner and reach the part that is moving. The snake strikes out at me, using its head like a fist, and I am knocked down. I try again, and again the head flies out of the darkness, banging into my chest. I grab blindly, and suddenly I have it and slash with my knife. There is a loud, hissing sound. I slash again and again; with a tremor the coils suddenly relax and Nance crawls free.

The snake slithers off slowly. Nance is breathing but in great pain.

'My ribs,' he moans. 'It crushed my ribs.'

Nance stretches out. Slowly his breathing returns to normal, but he is still in pain. After fifteen minutes he struggles to his feet, and we move on. The mosquitoes are still ferocious, but it seems to be cooler, and the noises coming from the depths of the forest – the cries of the monkeys and the screech of birds – have almost stopped.

It is impossible to tell how long we have been walking, for the moon has moved behind clouds, and the darkness is so absolute that I cannot see my watch.

Finally we sense a change in the air: it is perfectly still. Then, before we notice it, the darkness begins to fade. Slowly, shapes come into focus – leaves, ferns, the roots of trees. The forest is still dark, but a silver light is seeping into it.

'How much farther we got to go, Captain?' asks Nance. 'I gotta lie down – I can't keep goin' with this pain.'

I tell him it can't be much farther, that he should just hold on a little longer and we'll be there. But I know it isn't so. We've been walking a long time but the forest is endless, and there is no telling when we will come to the long house or even if we ever will. There are no landmarks, and even if there were we probably couldn't spot them. There's a good chance we will go right past the valley where the long house is – a better than even chance. Then nothing can help us, and we'll wander until we drop or someone or something gets us.

Ahead there is a clearing in the trees, and we make our way towards it. Nance is groaning with each step he takes, and I feel weak. Worst of all is the thirst. The forest is filled with rivers, but for some odd reason we have not encountered a single stream.

The clearing is on the side of a mountain and from it we can see a long way: there is nothing except more jungle-covered hills. We are completely lost. Nance must know as much, because he crouches down then stretches out on the ground. It does not look like he intends to move another step.

'We have to keep going,' I say. 'If we give up we're finished.'

'Where?' he asks. 'Captain, we ain't got the slightest idea which way to go.'

I lie down beside him. At least it is cool here. We can wait a while until our strength returns and then decide what to do. 'Montgomery,' I say to myself as I close my eyes, 'I hope you roast in hell.'

VII

The eyes are peering straight into mine; they have a curious expression, as if I were a creature from another planet. The face is a Dayak face. At least there is no white paint – we have that to be thankful for. Nance is awake too, but he is saying nothing. There must be a dozen of them squatting in a large circle with us in the centre. In their hands are blowguns and short spears tipped with the red substance that I know is deadly poison. But they do not look like they are hostile – the overwhelming emotion showing on their faces is curiosity.

'Nance,' I say, 'what do you make of this?'

'I don't think it's a war party, Captain.'

'I hope you're right,' I say. 'I just hope to God you're right.'

They have been listening to us, and now the one closest to me turns towards the man beside him and says something. There is a reply then everybody starts speaking at once in a wild jabber.

Nance and I sit up. At first they are so involved in their argument that nobody seems to notice; then one of them points to us and suddenly they are all quiet.

One begins to inch towards us. He has a peculiar expression on his face – a compound of curiosity and fear – and for the first time it dawns on me that they are as afraid of us as we are of them. Probably they have never seen a white man or a Negro before. We are exotic animals to them, and as long as we remain so we will probably be safe. When that changes then we will have to worry.

'Let's stand up and see what happens,' I say to Nance and we both stand.

They jump back and squat down, peering up at us out of confused, fear-filled eyes.

'We're going to brazen this out,' I say to Nance. 'It's the only way.'

I begin to make a motion as if I'm eating, but they only look confused. Then I rub my stomach and point to my mouth. Now they understand.

Several of them start babbling and point in a direction which I guess, by the position of the sun, lies to the north-east. 'They're either from the mountains or beyond,' I say. 'That's why they are acting like this. They've never seen men from the outside before.'

'What can we do?' Nance asks.

'We jolly them along,' I answer. 'Then, when the opportunity arises, we get away from them.'

He shakes his head.

'Got any other ideas?' I ask.

Now they are standing and pointing off towards the north-east. I nod to show that I understand, and we all begin to walk. Half of them are in front of us, half behind. Even though they're afraid of us they're taking no chances. I wonder how suspicious they are.

We walk through the afternoon and at sunrise make camp. Like the Kelabit, they are afraid of the dark and build a large fire. We squat around this and Nance and I watch them eat. They have no rice and instead eat something that looks like sweet potatoes and pieces of dried meat. They offer us some and, although the meat smells horrible, we eat it anyway. When they have finished eating they lie down and sleep, leaving two men as lookouts. We might be able to overpower these men and flee into the jungle, but it would be foolhardy. We have no idea where we are, and if we run from them it will indicate that we are afraid. That could prove fatal, for they could track us easily in the morning and once their awe of us is gone there is no telling what will happen.

I tell Nance all of this in whispers. He understands but is not keen about staying with them.

'The longer we're with them the farther we get from the Kelabit country,' he says. 'Once we get over those mountains we'll never get back.'

I know that he's probably right, but we'll have to chance it. The forest may be deadly, but if we're rested and have some food at least we'll have a chance. In the condition we're in now there is no hope of escaping.

53

With the first light of day they awaken and eat; then we start walking again. Nance and I are both sore. All night the mosquitoes feasted on us, plus a number of other insects of type unknown. The natives do not seem to be affected by this. Either they have rubbed something on their skin which functions as an insect repellant or their skin itself is as tough as leather.

All day we walk, stopping once to rest for about half an hour near noon, when the air is so hot that it seems to burn our lungs. We climb steadily, and the air becomes thinner and drier. Towards sunset, we cross a ridge and begin to descend, and I know that now we are on the north-western slopes of the Iran Mountains. We spend the night beside a small waterfall, lulled to sleep by the sound of cascading water. In the morning we press on and by noon have entered a broad valley. There is no cultivation here, but we begin to see people collecting roots or fishing in streams. Once we see a group of men carrying the carcase of a wild pig. By noon we reach their long house.

We are given a single room much like the one we each had in the Kelabit long house. This long house is more primitive, however, and not so clean. There is no porch outside the entrance: one climbs down a notched log and finds himself almost immediately in the jungle. The forest here is the same as that on the southern side of the slopes, but the life of the people seems harder. The food they give us is either half putrefied or nearly raw. The water they drink is fetid. The people themselves are not clean, and although physically they resemble the Kelabit, their manner seems rougher and more primitive.

Nance and I decide that we must wait a few days before we make our next move. Someone in this village should be able to give us an idea of where we are and how far and in what direction lies the land of the Kelabit. Once we have discovered this and provided ourselves with a cache of food, we will go. Until then we will bide our time.

The women in this long house are very direct. They flirt outrageously, and the first night of our stay is interrupted when four of them enter our room.

They stand over us and chatter to each other then squat in a circle and run their hands over our bodies. One of them starts to unbutton Nance's trousers but the others stop her; then, giggling, they leave.

We are exhausted and sleep like logs, waking late in the morning. Food has been provided, and we eat then climb down the notched log and explore the jungle in the vicinity of the long house.

The long house sits in the very centre of a valley. On both sides, densely forested hills rise almost to low-hanging clouds that form a roof above the valley. There is little sunlight, which is good because this keeps the heat down, but the insects are abundant – more abundant than on the southern side of the mountains. In addition to mosquitoes and flies there are tics and leeches and spiders of all sorts. Once we see a spider that is bigger than a human hand with all of the fingers extended. It is carrying what looks like a bird's egg, scuttling along the ground like a hairy crab.

And there are snakes. Nance is haunted by memories of the python; his ribs are still sore, and he shudders each time he sees a snake. Even on our short walk we see two pythons, curled in the lower branches of trees overhanging a small river that twists through the valley. These do not worry me as much as the smaller snakes, especially the ones that have brightly-coloured rings of red and gold circling them – these I know are highly poisonous.

We return to the long house when the sun is directly overhead. Food is brought to us by a young girl. It is roots and dried meat and a thick, brown liquid that is fermented. The smell is hideous but we consume everything. It amazes me that we do not become sick; apparently our constitutions have toughened, and I make a joke, saying that now we'll even be able to stand navy chow. Nance laughs at this. He is feeling more optimistic now. For a while he was down, but he's got a core of iron.

In the afternoon we sleep and when evening comes, more food is brought to us. We have seen plenty of women but few men other than those who brought us to this place. There have to be more men living in the long house, and the only reason I think of for there being so few present is that the others are away, probably hunting – either for animals or human heads.

After we eat we lie down. The sounds of the jungle fill the night – the screeches of monkeys and the cries of birds. We have drunk some more of the fermented liquid and we are both a little groggy. Half in a dream, I see the women reappear. This time there are at least a dozen of them. They stand above us in a circle and giggle, their white teeth glittering in the flickering light of a torch that one of them has brought.

Then it begins. They do not even bother to remove their sarongs, instead merely hike them up about their waists. Several of them hold us down while others remove our clothes; then we are manipulated until we are erect. This seems to amuse them. They are especially interested in Nance, who is quite large.

After we are erect they ride us, one after the other. After the first slides up and down until I climax, another takes her place. When she finishes I am flaccid, but the women take something from a bowl and rub it on my penis. It smells like cloves and gives a strange tingling sensation, and as I look down my organ swells and stands. Then another climbs on.

Each of the women has both of us. I know that in the morning I will be very sore, but now there is only a feeling of tingling numbness. I have stopped ejaculating, but still each time the paste is rubbed on my penis, it stands erect.

I am half delirious, for they have been giving me the fermented liquid to drink, continuously pouring it down my throat while they slide up and down on my penis. All of my being – all my sensation – seems concentrated in my penis. The last thing I recall before I lose consciousness is hearing Nance moan, whether in ecstasy or pain I cannot tell.

In the morning we sleep late, but when we finally awake we find no food. This is strange, so I rise and walk stiffly to the doorway and push back the screen. The hallway that runs down the centre of the long house is completely deserted, but I can hear the buzz of a voice somewhere outside. I walk towards the entrance, but some instinct prompts me to stay inside. I crouch down and peer out.

There is a small clearing just beyond the long house, a circular place ringed by the forest. All the people of the long house are standing here. I notice at a glance that there are many more than I had noticed before: the men who have been missing since our arrival have returned. But it is not these people who attract my attention: it is the men standing in front of them. These men are Japanese soldiers and one of them is talking to the natives.

VIII

To escape is impossible; there is nothing to do but wait and see what will happen. It does not take long to find out, for within minutes the Japanese soldiers are standing before the doorway to our room, rifles in hand, staring at us with the superior, malicious smiles they reserve for stupid Americans who have not reckoned on their ultimate victory.

None of them seems to know English, for they do not try to question us, but instead tie our hands behind our backs and post a guard.

Late in the day two women appear with food. They speak to each other but avoid the eyes of the soldiers, who seem to be ogling them. It's clear that they view these men with a certain amount of contempt. They point to our bound hands which make it impossible for us to eat, but the soldiers merely shrug. One of the women leaves, then returns in a few minutes with some fruit and bowls filled with the fermented liquid that was poured down us last night. Then they begin to feed us.

The Japanese soldiers watch what is happening very closely but make no move to stop the women. One of them prods one of the women with his bayonet and she turns on him, loosing a stream of abuse that shocks us with its vehemence. The man eyes her sullenly but does nothing.

When the women leave we sleep. We are surprised that the Japanese remain in this place. It would be more logical for them to return with us to their base camp – there would be men who could question us there. We don't have long to wait to discover the reason why they remain.

He is a short man, very near-sighted, with thick glasses that make his eyes appear like pinpoints of light glowing evilly in his yellow face. He cannot be taller than five foot four, and he looks like he weighs about a hundred and ten pounds. But his English is very good and he is not stupid. As he speaks I try to place the accent. There is a certain nasality and now and then an intrusive 'r', almost like someone from Boston might have.

The little man asks us questions for an hour. The answers he gets cannot please him, but it is difficult to tell this because the expression on his face remains constant; the eyes blink at us, the lips curl at the corners in an expression that might be a smile. We say we have been flying from Port Moresby to Calcutta and that we had to ditch our plane somewhere in the jungle. We compliment him on the efficiency of the Japanese fighter pilots: were it not for their skill we would be in New Delhi now, sitting in the shade beside a swimming pool, sipping a tall, cool drink.

Now the short man really smiles, showing a set of buck teeth which make him look like the Japanese villains in the patriotic war movies they bored everyone on shipboard with, night after night. This man could be played by Peter Lorre. I wonder if he will live up to his looks.

After two hours another man joins the questioner. He is tall for a Japanese, with an attractive, strikingly handsome face. He and the short man discuss something and then he leaves.

Now the procedure changes. Each time a question is asked and no answer given the short man nods to one of the guards, and he thumps us hard in the ribs with his rifle butt. At first the pain is tolerable, but soon the repeated blows begin to weaken us. It feels as if my ribs have been crushed to a pulp, and every time I draw a breath the pain is almost unbearable. I want to cry out, but I won't do this. I don't want to let the little man know I am weakening.

If it's bad for me, it's much worse for Nance, because his ribs have already been injured by the python. I watch his face: there are beads of sweat on his forehead and the corner of his mouth is twitching.

Abruptly, the short man stops questioning us, nods to the guards, and leaves. We slump to the ground. For several minutes neither of us speaks. Finally I ask Nance how he feels.

'I can't take much more, Captain,' he says, his eyes squinted with pain.

'We could tell him a crock,' I say, 'that might hold him for a while – at least until he gets a chance to check it out. It would buy us time.'

'If he starts again I'll have to tell him something,' Nance says. 'Every time that guy bangs me in the ribs it feels like somebody's drivin' a spear right through me.'

In less than an hour the little man returns. With him is the handsome man. This time they have apparently already decided upon their strategy, for the questioning begins without any discussion. Nance struggles for ten minutes, but then he doubles over and starts moaning. The little man calls for another guard, and Nance is held down while one of the men works over his ribs with his boot. Nance screams each time he is kicked.

'We're reconnaissance men,' he moans. 'We were sent here to learn about troop deployment.'

Evidently this is what they want to hear, for I can see the expressions on their faces change, and the little man and the handsome man exchange glances. They ask Nance how he reached this long house, underlining their question with another kick in the ribs.

'We were dropped into the jungle twenty miles to the north,' he mutters, his voice so weak that it is barely audible.

'How were you to get out?' asks the little man, his eyes glittering like a ferret's.

'We were gonna make our way on foot to the Rajang River and from there by boat to the coast. A PT boat was going to pick us up at the river's mouth.'

'Rendezvous place and time!' snaps the little man.

Nance does not answer him. The man nods to the guards again; this time they give Nance a half dozen kicks. He begins to whimper pitifully.

'June twenty-third,' he says. 'At twenty-two hundred hours, latitude 2° 29' 40" N longitude 111° 7' 25" E.'

He's convincing enough to be an actor; even I half believe him.

The Japs talk for a few minutes then the officers leave. Nance is lying face down. He is still whimpering, and I ask him if there is anything I can do. He shakes his head.

The day begins to die, and the light from outside turns gold. We want to sleep but the pain won't let us. Two men are guarding the entranceway; from time to time they peer in to

check on us. Night has almost fallen when the women appear
again. They look at Nance; then one of them leaves and returns
in a few minutes with a very old man carrying a sack. He feels
Nance's ribs then takes some ferns from his sack and rubs them
between his palms until they are crushed into a paste. This he
rubs gently over Nance's back and sides. Finally he unwinds a
long strip of cloth and wraps it around Nance until he looks like
a mummy from the waist up. The women give us some food,
and we eat slowly. It's painful to swallow, but I know I have to
eat if I want to keep up my strength. Nance can only drink
some of the fermented liquid.

The old man watches the women feed us, and when they
have finished the three of them rise and leave. I watch the
women's eyes. When they look towards the soldiers there is an
expression I have never seen in these people before – it is not
wariness nor is it hate but something else, a kind of passionless,
indifferent assessment such as one might make if one were
looking at a rock or a plant.

It is night and the rain is falling and there is a strong wind.
Nance and I are remembering the things we have heard about
the Japanese POW camps. It is said that of every two men who
enter them only one survives. There is no way of telling how
long the war will last, but it does not look like it will end soon.
Neither of us is looking forward to spending the next five years
starving to death in a pest hole presided over by men like those
who have been questioning us. We have to get out of here – to
make a break for it – and we have to do it soon. But we don't
have any food and we're battered and we don't even know
which direction to go in.

'We ain't got a chance, Captain,' says Nance. 'Even if we
reach the jungle the bastards will probably be able to track us –
and if they don't get us the jungle will.'

'What do you think they'll do when they discover that what
you told them isn't true?' I ask. 'They won't stop until they find
out what they want. The choice we'll have then is either to be
live traitors or dead patriots – that's a no-win proposition.'

Towards midnight the rain begins to fall harder, drumming
on the roof of the long house like small bullets. Nance sleeps,
but I am restless and slept out. It is pitch dark and I cannot see
the man guarding us, but I know where he is. Sometime earlier

in the night one of the sentries left and was not replaced. Either they are not worried about us trying to escape or they are getting lax. And this sentry is asleep – I can hear him snoring.

Suddenly my ears prick up: somebody has come into the hallway. The steady tattoo of the rain is loud and the new sound is different, softer: it's the sound bare feet make on the palm-leaf covered floor of the hall. A man who wasn't listening for the sound would never have heard it, but I was – I knew they would come. The expression in the eyes of the women who brought our food told me this.

Then they are inside the room untying our hands and feet. There are two of them. We cannot see their faces in the darkness. They whisper something in our ears which I can't understand then lead us out of the room and down the darkened hallway. The sentry has not stirred; probably his food or water was drugged.

Outside it is almost as dark as within, but in the faint yellowish glow that reflects off the low-hanging clouds I can see their faces: the two who brought us food. They look frightened and one of them keeps looking towards the entrance of the long house, as if she were afraid that the Japanese soldiers will appear. The women give each of us large sacks containing fruit and rice and pieces of dried meat. The soldiers have taken our guns, but the women give us primitive machetes so that we can hack our way through the forest.

We stand in the clearing before the forest, pelted by the rain, and look anxiously towards the south-east. That's the direction we have to go in, but neither of us really wants to venture into the jungle. The women leave us. Nance shakes his head.

'It ain't possible, Captain,' he says. 'It just ain't possible.'

An hour before I was certain but now I feel as he does. There is a sudden crash of thunder and then lightning ripples across the sky, illuminating the clearing. Two men are standing in the entranceway of the long house, staring at us. They are wearing uniforms and carrying rifles. Before they can raise them and sight we have reached the edge of the forest and are plunging ahead, tearing and cutting our way through vines and leaves, hoping that in the blackness of the night and the depths of the forest we can lose our pursuers.

All night we travel and when dawn comes we are in a deep valley, making our way along the banks of a roaring stream. The vegetation is thinner here and we can make good time. From the position of the sun, my guess is that we are heading almost due south. This is not where we want to go but we have no choice. If we plunge into the jungle our progress will slow to a crawl and we will not be able to see the sun – in such circumstances it will be almost impossible to move in a set direction.

As we walk we continually look over our shoulders. The stream twists and turns like a snake, and visibility to the rear extends only about thirty yards. Still we have to look: our nerves will not let us alone. We know that the Japanese are back there somewhere. Several times we have heard noises in the distance – noises that men make when they are cutting through undergrowth. We are both spooky, but we don't think that we are so spooky that we imagined those noises.

We have been eating the fruit the woman gave us and drinking water from the stream. The water is refreshing, but already we have been plagued by the runs so that our strength is ebbing. The air is humid, almost viscous, and we are moving at a good pace so we are panting too. Nance's ribs are hurting him but he says nothing. Each time he takes a breath, however, I can see him wince.

The water in the stream is startlingly cold. That means it has come from high up on the mountains. It is rushing fast, and the land seems to be descending steadily. My guess is that we are now on the southern slopes of the Iran Mountains, but there is no way to know this for sure. We have never reached the top of a mountain where we had a view over the surrounding country. The stream has been following a valley that cuts through the mountains, and we have been following the stream for almost eight hours, ever since we first stumbled upon it in the darkness.

We both would like to stop and rest but we cannot risk this. Every minute is precious. The Japanese are relentless, and we know that, if they catch us, whatever treatment we have had at their hands so far will seem like a honeymoon compared to what they will do. 'We burnt our bridges,' I tell Nance, and he frowns and forces himself to go a little faster.

This part of the forest is remarkably empty of wild life. We have seen only a few birds but otherwise nothing that moves except insects and an occasional snake – no monkeys or wild pigs or deer. It is ominously quiet and this is unsettling, for always before the jungle was filled with noise. I cannot understand this. It is as if the part of the jungle we are now passing through were cursed or blighted in some curious way.

Late in the afternoon the valley suddenly narrows. Here the sides of the mountains drop sheer. The scene is eerie. The sun has almost sunk behind the horizon to the west, but a few golden rays still light the eastern side of the valley, while the western side is in total darkness. The valley is very straight here and seems to run on for miles, like a great chute. Now at last we begin to see wildlife again – flocks of small white birds with crimson-tipped wings. They fly back and forth, from one side of the valley to the other, as if they were fleeing some ghostly predator. There is a soft but steady wind blowing from the north so that the leaves look like a gently rippling green sea.

The valley becomes so narrow that we have to wade in the stream. Our feet are cold and we shiver in the humid air. We are dead tired but we keep moving, lurching and sometimes nearly falling as we make our way over slippery rocks. Night has fallen now and our bodies are crying out for rest, but we keep plunging ahead. We will travel through the night, following the stream. With luck by morning we should be out of the mountains.

Suddenly Nance stops and grips my arm. 'Look, Cap!' he whispers, his voice hoarse with tension.

I have been walking with my head down for a long time or I would surely have noticed before now: ahead and behind, on both sides of the hill, is a cluster of gold lights, flickering in the darkness.

We don't move and for several minutes the lights remain stationary; then slowly they begin to bounce and move around. By now I know what they are – torches – and in a few minutes we will know who is carrying them, because they are converging on us.

At a distance of thirty yards they stop moving. We can see figures holding the torches but only dimly. There must be about fifty of them.

'What are they doing?' Nance asks.

'I don't know – probably sizing us up,' I say.

Now they are moving again, a step at a time, cautiously, all together as men do who need the support of one another to confront something that frightens them.

We can see them more clearly now. Superficially they appear like the Kelabit, but they seem to be slighter.

When they have reached a point ten yards from us they stop again. They have formed a circle around us, which is brightly lighted by their torches. The expression on their faces is one of awe – obviously they have never seen any men like us before. Finally one man inches forward and reaches out to touch me. I let him do this. It is my skin that fascinates him, together with my GI fatigues. He touches the cloth and rubs it between his fingers, like a tailor. Now more of them, made bold by this man, do the same. They are carrying knives thrust in a kind of belt that is wrapped around their waists – otherwise they are stark naked. The language in which they are chattering to each other is totally unlike the language of the Kelabit.

'What do you think these people want?' Nance asks.

I tell him that I don't know but that the best thing we can do is just wait and see.

'Don't make any sudden moves,' I say. 'So far they seem friendly.'

They begin to move off towards the side of the valley now, with us in their midst. The tree-covered walls of the valley are steep here, towering far above us, but there is a path that winds upward and we follow it, climbing until we reach the lip of the cliff then striking out across a plain. The moonlight is bright and we can see numerous copses of trees spread across the plain, and in the distance – ten or fifteen miles – some mountain peaks covered with more forest.

We walk at a good pace for twenty minutes; then a crater suddenly yawns before us, immensely deep and so wide that I cannot see the other side of it. There is a path here, weaving and twisting back and forth as it descends into the darkness below. We are led down this, while a few men rush ahead. Somewhere far below, more torches are winking in the darkness.

It takes us another fifteen minutes to reach the floor of the crater. Here we are met by a mob of people, all carrying torches. We are led to a large open space, a sort of square, in the middle of a dozen buildings. The buildings themselves are only raised platforms covered with roofs and open on all sides. The people surround us, and in the centre of them, seated on carved stools, are half a dozen old men. These seem to be the elders and leaders.

The old men speak; probably they are asking us questions. We understand nothing that they say, but finally, by gesture, manage to tell them that we have come from the north. Now that we have been around them for a while I begin to notice the differences between them and the Kelabit. These people are definitely smaller. Their faces are broad and their skin is darker; there is something almost negroid in the cast of their features. They seem gentle, yet each carries a large dagger. Even the women are naked. They peer at us but keep at a distance, as if they are afraid of us. Most of all what seems to puzzle them is the difference in the colour of Nance and me. They keep pointing from one of us to the other then talking very fast.

We are led to one of the buildings and given a place to sit down. The floor of the building is covered with a primitive woven mat. The people gather round and stare at us. We are both dead tired and all we want is sleep. Almost all. Before we can sleep we have to relieve ourselves, but with all these people around there doesn't seem to be any discreet way of doing this. It's peculiar how a man's training, especially in that area of his life, can never be quite forgotten. All we have to do is step off the platform and move to the part of the clearing near the trees; already we have seen several of the natives do this, but we cannot bring ourselves to follow suit.

Finally I stand.

'We can't wait all night, Nance,' I say. 'I'm going to take a crap and if they want to watch then let them.'

I walk towards the edge of the clearing and the crowd follows me. By now they must have some inkling of what I'm going to do, but they do not move away, and when I unbuckle then lower my pants I can see their eyes following my movements.

Because they're watching, it takes me a long time. When I finish and pull up my pants, I can hear them talking excitedly to one another. I'm not sure, but I think that seeing me defecate has reassured them that there is a relationship between us – that in certain very basic ways we are constructed the same. Until they saw me lower my pants they probably weren't quite sure of this, but now they are, and when Nance follows me they watch him too.

Now I can see smiles on their faces and chuckles and nods of the head.

Once back on the platform we fall almost instantly asleep. There is no screen or netting of any kind, but, surprisingly, there are not many mosquitoes. In this instance, however, it probably makes little difference. I don't think I have ever been quite so tired before.

IX

Life is hard in this place. The people are much more primitive than the Kelabit. Their houses are uncomfortable and poorly-made, and the food they offer to share with us is barely edible. Few of them, not even the young men, are strong or robust. However they are friendly and amazingly sensitive to our feelings. They soon realize that it unsettles us when they follow us around, so they leave us to ourselves although their curiosity is almost overpowering.

The children are forever smiling and waving to us, and they watch our every move. Nance is their favourite. He is much taller than any man they have ever seen, and they regard him as a sort of superman. To entertain them he performs feats of strength, lifting large logs or carrying several of them on his shoulders at one time. The adults are still a little afraid of us, but the children have absolutely no fear, and they tumble about and climb over us as if we were the family mutts.

We are probably safe in this place. The country is a trackless maze of valleys and mountains, and the only way to travel in it is to follow a river or a stream. This is how the natives travel and the Japanese must do the same. This crater is so far from a large stream that the likelihood of somebody stumbling upon it is nil. It might be possible to observe it from the air, but even that would be difficult, for it is very deep and a large part of it lies in shadow for most of the day; if an observer wanted to peer into the crater he would have to fly almost down into it, hovering like a hummingbird as he did so. No reconnaissance plane can do that.

I still cannot discover how the natives intercepted us. They seemed to know we were coming, for how else can their presence in such numbers so far from their home be explained? Sometimes lone men or a fishing or hunting party leaves the crater, but never a group as large as the one that intercepted us and never at night. If I could only understand them then I could ask, but their language, a strange collection of whistles and guttural clicks, is completely beyond me. We are picking up occasional words, but except for these, which allow us to fulfil very basic needs, we have no way of communicating with these people.

The elders talk to us every day. We are summoned by one of the men – the women are kept far from us – and led to the largest building in the village. Here the old men sit in state under a roof made of loosely woven palm leaves. The sun is blindingly bright and hot – so hot that walking only a few hundred feet in it makes a man perspire freely. The old men greet us heartily and invite us to sit on one of the crude stools they use. Then a large clay bowl containing a putrid liquid is passed around. Invariably, this makes Nance and me gag, but we force it down. The taste is not bad, but the smell is peculiarly offensive, almost like rotten potatoes.

After everybody has drunk, the old men begin to speak. Mostly they talk and we listen. They are fond of long monologues, during which they move their hands in grandiose gestures and thump their chests. Nance and I nod at what we consider the proper moment. Each time one of the old men finishes talking, we say a few words, which they listen to with rapt expressions. Then we fall silent and another man speaks. The entire process lasts for almost two hours; then once more the putrid liquid is passed around and we take a final draught.

Afterwards, Nance and I are both very sleepy. It may be the heat or perhaps the fatigue of sitting and listening to people make sounds that are totally meaningless to us. The liquid is not alcoholic, but it upsets our stomachs and aggravates the diarrhoea that has been weakening us. We are both having difficulty regaining our strength. The food is wretched and although there are few mosquitoes, there is a myriad of other insects that plague us throughout the night, so that we never seem able to sleep for more than a few hours at a time. There are spiders and ants and beetles of all kinds, big and little, of a million different colours and shapes, and each of them seems to take a special delight in feasting on us. I tell Nance that this is because we're a novelty. 'They've never tasted American blood before,' I say. 'These bugs are gourmets – they like foreign flesh.'

Nance doesn't think this is very funny. His ribs have healed, but his dysentery is much worse than mine; at least a dozen times a day he must duck into the shadows of the trees behind the houses and relieve himself, and each time he feels weaker.

'If we stay here much longer,' he says, 'I'll be a skeleton.'

I tell him to be patient. At least there are no Japanese soldiers, and as long as we're here we don't have to worry about somebody taking our heads. Nance appreciates that. The first few days we spent here we searched for signs of heads but there were none. By now, neither of us is very worried – these people seem too gentle to fear.

'In a few days we'll make a break for it,' I tell him. 'I don't think they'll stop us, but there's no sense in going just yet. We've got to wait until more of our strength returns.'

Neither of us feels ready for the jungle – we remember the countless forested hills, the snakes and mosquitoes and the feeling of complete and absolute frustration as we wandered aimlessly from valley to valley, never knowing if we were headed in the right direction. At least in this place we feel secure.

Early this morning a large hunting party assembled and left the crater. We have seen this happen before and thought nothing of it, but night has come and the hunting party has not returned, and now there is lamentation in the village. Women wail and a drum is beaten slowly and a ritual dance performed. The women sit in two rows, facing each other, and men dance up and down before them in an unending procession. They take slow, shuffling steps and hang their heads, as if they are ashamed; then, slowly, the speed of the procession increases and the men begin to chant in unison with the women. They move faster and faster until they are almost running and the chanting is a roar. Finally, the men collapse in exhaustion and crawl off to their pallets and fall asleep. The women remain seated, and all through the night the air is filled with their mournful wails.

Towards noon the next day two of the party return. They are badly battered – one has a gaping head wound and the other a gash that has completely disabled one arm. The villagers gather round and listen as they tell their story. A council is held and the elders debate the situation, but already, while they are speaking, the course of action has been determined, for Nance and I can see women gathering family belongings together and moving out of the village. Soon all follow them.

The place they march to is at the far end of the crater. Here the wall of the crater is sheer and rocky, with almost no vegetation. A narrow path barely wide enough for a single man is carved in it, zigzagging upward for several hundred feet until it stops abruptly at a point about two-thirds of the way to the top. From the floor of the crater it is difficult to see the end of the path clearly because of the angle, but it looks like the mouth of a cave exists there.

The people start up the path. They are carrying baskets of food and great jugs of water. Babies are strapped to the backs of the women.

Women and children go first, then the old people. The men remain at the bottom, peering anxiously back towards the village and the tree-covered cliff behind it.

Almost half the people have reached the top of the path and disappeared into the cave when a man appears beneath the trees opposite the village, where the path from the plain above opens into the crater floor. He is running very fast.

The people cry out and begin to climb faster, scrambling up the perilously narrow path. Parcels of food and jugs of water are dropped and smashed to bits on the crater floor. The men form a large semi-circle two-deep around the bottom of the path, each holding a machete.

The man who appeared from beneath the trees has almost reached us now. He is yelling and pointing back towards the far side of the crater, and now all the men peer intently in that direction, as if, at any time, they expected to see a legion of devils appear.

And then I see them. They come out of the trees near the village and stand in a group. Slowly their number swells until there must be a hundred of them. Even at this distance – it is five or six hundred yards – I know that I have seen men like this before. Their faces are painted white and the long knives they carry flash in the sun.

How much time passes is hard to tell, for when a man is truly frightened time plays tricks, and I am filled with terror because I know too well what these white-faced men seek.

They trot towards us, holding small round shields before them. The men around me stand firm. They do not even have bows and arrows, only the machetes they hold in their hands and the knowledge that if they cannot hold back these onrushing men with the white faces their wives and children will be slaughtered.

The path behind us is clear now, and we both begin to scramble up it. Nance and I are in the middle of the men and halfway up the face of the crater when the attackers reach the bottom of the path. There are still a dozen men there and they fight valiantly, holding the onrushing warriors back for a few minutes before they are overwhelmed.

The attacking party begins to ascend the path. Almost a hundred feet separates the last of the villagers from the first of the white-faced raiders, but the distance is decreasing rapidly, for the path narrows as it climbs, and the people at the top near the cave must move slowly.

Half the attacking party deploys at the base of the cliff and shoots arrows at us. The distance is great and most of these bounce harmlessly off the rocks. We have almost reached the mouth of the cave now. We can see the face of an old man peering anxiously down at us from the small opening. There are ten villagers below us on the path, the last two turned to face the onrushing attackers. Then there is twenty-five yards of empty pathway, then the first of the men with white faces.

'We're going to make it, Captain!' Nance yells. 'We're going to make it!'

The first of the attackers goes down on one knee and raises the long tube he has been carrying to his mouth, and a dart flies past our heads. More and more darts come, buzzing through the air like a swarm of attacking hornets. Already our rearguard – the last two men in our party – have been hit. For a moment they stand their ground, bracing themselves and leaning back against the cliff. But then they go limp and fall forward into space where they plummet down, arms and legs akimbo like grotesque rag dolls.

Just above us the path zags back in the opposite direction, giving the men on the path below a clear shot at anybody ascending, but where we stand is screened from them by an outcropping of rock so that the darts fly harmlessly past. If we can hold this place we will be safe, but we dare not advance farther.

Nance and I work our way back down the path to the rear of the party; we are bigger and stronger than the villagers and have a better chance of holding off the raiders than they do. We flatten ourselves against the rock face of the cliff and wait. We can see the rest of the attacking party far below, watching and shouting instructions to men who are climbing towards us.

A man appears around the rock outcropping, his shield raised and brandishing a long, curved knife. He is coming very fast, almost running, hoping that his momentum will enable him to overpower us. I crouch low and take the brunt of his charge on my shoulder then lurch upward. Nance grabs my belt from the rear to keep me from flying outward into space.

The man is upended and flies over my shoulder, bounces against the cliff wall, then careens outward, screaming as he falls to his death. I crouch down and wait for the next raider.

In a moment he appears; he does not charge but instead raises his blowgun and shoots a dart at me. It flies over my head but hits a man behind us who collapses, but others grab him so that he does not fall. The attacker reaches into a pouch at his belt and removes another dart, but before he can load it into the pipe I have reached him and flipped him into space. He spins crazily, clawing at the air as he falls.

Several minutes pass but nothing happens. The attacking party holds a meeting, from which, after a few minutes, half a dozen men break and cross to the village and the pathway beyond, where they disappear into the trees.

The sun is hot and beats down unmercifully, but there is nothing to do except remain where we are. Raiders are still waiting just around the outcropping of rock and if we try to ascend, they will shoot us with darts. When darkness falls our chances will be better, but still they will be able to hear us, and at close range even a blind shot will be dangerous. I don't know what we would gain by reaching the cave anyway. With no one to block the path, the raiding party will be able to climb to the entrance *en masse*, and it would then be an easy matter for them to force their way in. Right here, at least their superiority in numbers is negated.

The sun has begun to sink towards the western horizon and the heat has let up a little when I am jarred out of a half trance by a shout from above. At the same time there is a rumbling noise and a huge rock careens past. The other men in our party press themselves flat against the side of the cliff. More and more rocks fly past, skipping wildly as they bounce off the wall of the cliff. One of the men in our party is struck and tumbles forward into space, then another. A rock crashes into my arm and it goes numb.

Nance has been hit on the shoulder, and there is a big gash in his forehead.

'They're on the lip of the crater!' I yell. 'They can't reach us from there but they're trying to bomb us.'

'They're doing a good job,' says Nance.

Now more rocks come, mixed with a hail of darts. Soon men will try to come around the outcropping again. They know we have been weakened and that now is the time to take us, before darkness makes it more difficult for them to move quickly and easier for us to ascend unseen.

More rocks rain down; this time they are hardly bigger than the size of a fist. The men at the top of the cliff must have used all the large rocks that were at hand and are running out of ammunition. I hear more shouts from above, answered a moment later from the party at the base of the cliff. They will come now, I know it, and I move into a crouch, my eyes glued on the rock outcropping.

Two of them come this time, one after the other, rushing with drawn knives. I block the first but my strength is ebbing and I cannot fling him outward. I have one hand on his wrist, the other round his throat. For a moment we balance precariously, like dancers; then our centre of gravity suddenly swings outward and I can feel myself begin to fall and release my grip on the attacker and grab for the edge of the ledge. He does the same but a split second too late and manages to grasp the ledge with only one hand. A second before he loses his grip he twists his head and looks at me. Time has stopped, and for a moment we are locked together in eternity; then his grip loosens and he plunges downward, dropping like a stone. Immediately, two strong hands grab my arm and I am jerked back to the pathway.

Nance has lifted me up, but I do not have time to thank him, for they are coming again. This time we meet them as a team, driving the first man backward until he collides with the man behind him. But these men are stronger than the last two, for they quickly right themselves and come on again.

The lead man slashes and I feel his knife tear through my shirt and rip into the skin of my chest. Instinctively, I kick out and catch him in the groin with my foot. He doubles up, and I club him with a right cross and he flies outward into space. Nance and the second man are grappling. The man slashes with his knife and Nance leaps out of the way then makes a lunge for him. The man is agile and Nance cannot reach him. Again and again the scenario is repeated – the man slashing at Nance who avoids his thrust and then lunges futilely. But with each repetition Nance is slowing down, and the attacker's thrusts are coming closer and closer.

I move towards them, hoping to draw the man's attention from Nance. At that moment, a sudden barrage of rocks rains down on us again. Nance is struck on the forehead and goes down. The white-faced man presses himself flush against the rock face; then, when the barrage has ended, he advances on Nance, now lying unconscious.

I grab a rock and fling it at the attacker. It catches him in the middle of the back and he lurches forwards, almost losing his balance, then he regains it and turns towards me.

He comes on, holding his knife before him. This man is taller and stronger-looking than any of the raiders we have battled with so far. His eyes are fierce and unafraid. I can feel blood oozing out of the wound in my chest, but I am still strong and alert. The man steps forward and slashes. I leap out of the way. He advances and I back up. He looks even stronger now, more certain of himself. He knows that if he can keep forcing me backwards he will drive us from this particular spot, where we can hold back the attacking party indefinitely. If he can back me up ten more feet and hold me at bay until some of his cohorts join him he will have accomplished his goal.

I stand my ground and he stops. We stare into each other's eyes, each man judging the other, looking for a sign, trying to tell just how much courage the other has. Then he comes on again, this time swinging the knife slowly back and forth in front of him. I fake a roundhouse punch to the jaw, at the same time kicking out for his legs. He goes for the feint and does not see the kick coming. It knocks him off balance only for a second but that's all I need. Now I've got the wrist of his knife hand with both of my hands, and I twist it violently down and out. There is a crack and he screams in agony. I kick out again, catching him in the groin; he doubles up and I swing an uppercut, starting it down low and putting all the power I can muster into it.

The punch stuns him before it lifts him off the ground and over the ledge, so that he plummets downward limply, relaxed, a man going peacefully to his final rest.

Nance and I are alone on the path again. If there are any more of the attacking party behind the outcropping they have decided to wait us out. The other villagers have all climbed to safety in the cave above. The sun is sinking fast; already it is half gone behind the horizon. Soon night will come and with it the attackers' next move.

We can see a fire glowing at the base of the cliff. Around it sit the attacking party, legs crossed, backs straight like meditating Buddhas. The night is perfectly still. We have been watching them for half an hour. The fire was built carefully, started with small twigs, larger branches added, until now it is roaring. Above it is a skewer that holds pieces of sizzling meat. The aroma rises, filling the air with an obscene perfume. The smell is not strong nor particularly offensive but it nauseates us, for we have seen the white-faced men butcher the corpses of the villagers they killed at the base of the cliff, dress the meat, and place several pieces of it on the skewer. We know that the people in the cave above have seen this too, and we can imagine the terror they feel. The sensation that watching men prepare human flesh for eating creates in another human being is uncanny. It sends chills running up and down my spine, and I can feel each hair stand on end.

When the men begin to eat the sensation intensifies and I begin to feel nauseous; then suddenly I go numb. I watch the men eat but I have absolutely no feeling. My mind has left this body and this place. I still watch the men beneath me, but their reality is gone – they are not men but things, and what they are doing, the eating of human flesh, is only a physical action – a kind of dumb show or pantomime without emotional import.

How long this sensation endures I don't know, but eventually something inside me snaps and I come back to myself, drenched with sweat and gasping for breath.

Weird howls fill the night. The men below have begun a chaotic chant, as if each were conversing with his own private demon. It is a forlorn sound, a chorus of wails that gives me a feeling of utter and complete desolation. I tell myself that what I have witnessed is a custom, a primitive rite, and that it can have no significance to me. I am a civilized man; these people are savages. My concepts of good and bad, virtue and evil, have no meaning in their world. I reason that the overwhelming horror I feel is because suddenly the veneer deposited by a few thousand years of civilization has been pierced and my civilized sensibilities outraged. But these thoughts do not lessen the feeling of doom that has settled over me.

There are whispers behind us and we turn. I have dozed off with my back pressed flat against the rock wall of the cliff. How long I have been out I don't know, but the sounds came from higher up on the path – the direction in which the villagers would have come from. I hear them again. We cannot see them clearly in the darkness, but they seem to be the largest of the villagers.

'We've got to go up to the cave,' Nance says. 'These guys can hold out until we're rested enough to come back.'

'Are you sure they'll stay here?' I ask.

'There's no telling, Captain. I think they will but we can't count on anything.'

I'm tired or I wouldn't be quibbling. The fact is, we need rest or we'll be useless.

It takes us fifteen minutes to climb up to the cave. At the end the going is difficult – the path is not only narrow but steep. That the old people and children were able to climb it amazes me.

The cave is filled with people. It is narrow but very deep. The people line the walls, sitting in family groups. Most are sleeping but the council of elders is awake, waiting for Nance and me. They ask questions which we cannot understand, but soon it becomes clear that they somehow believe the danger of the attackers can be magicked away with words, because they talk on and on, while Nance and I doze off. I want to tell them to waken us just before dawn but don't know how to do this. Finally I scratch a picture of the rising sun on the cave floor and they nod. In a moment I am asleep.

I open my eyes sleepily then leap to my feet. The sun is already half over the horizon to the east and the sky is bright with early morning light. I wake Nance and we scramble down the path.

As we move I peer anxiously towards the floor of the crater: there is no sign of the raiders. They must have already started up the pathway.

We rush on, expecting to meet them head on at any moment. When we reach the rock outcropping, the four men who relieved us are still standing guard, squatting like watchdogs, knives drawn. We join them and wait. My heart is pounding and I am dripping sweat, shivering in the cool morning air.

Two hawks circle lazily over the village, searching for their morning meal. The sun is clear of the horizon now, but long shadows still cover most of the crater. The breeze has died and there is perfect silence. I listen intently. If there were a large number of men approaching, no matter how silently they would come, there would be some noise. Nothing.

Cautiously, we stand and make our way past the outcropping. Once on the other side we can see the path all the way to the floor of the crater. No one. They have gone, probably at the first light of dawn, and the only signs of them are the blackened coals of their fire and the spit where they roasted their victims.

X

'We'll have to go it alone,' I tell Nance.

'That's a mighty big jungle,' Nance says.

'We'll make out all right,' I say, but I'm not so sure. If I were, we would already be on our way.

'If one of the villagers could guide us we would have a better chance,' he says.

'That's why we spent the afternoon talking to the elders,' I say. 'But we are making no progress. They don't want us to go because they think we have powerful medicine – that the next time the raiders come looking for heads we will be able to protect them again.'

'They won't help us then,' says Nance.

'No,' I say, shaking my head. 'They're like a bunch of politicians – home turf comes first with them.'

'We better stay, Cap,' says Nance.

It's the first time I've heard him say anything like that, and I decide I'd better not let it stand.

'No, we go,' I say. 'We weren't sent here to play god for these people – we were sent here to get that priest out and that's what we're going to do.'

Nance doesn't answer right away. He's thinking and he must have come to the conclusion that the logic of silence is on his side. With words he cannot beat me, he knows that, but while he's quiet we feel the heat of the sun and hear the never-ending buzz of a million insects. When there's silence the jungle dominates, an unending sea of leaves and vines just waiting to swallow us up.

'We can't stay here forever, Nance,' I say, cutting into that

silence with words, the tools of my world. 'We ought to face it
–we were lucky the last time, that's all. Those raiders will
return – if not next week or the week after, then next month or
the month after that. This time we had a stroke of luck. If we
hadn't met them on that path – in that *one* place on the path –
our heads would be hanging above the entranceway of their
long house right now. We aren't any safer here than we would
be in the jungle. If we stay here the chances of us ever getting
out are zero. You think anybody from the outside world is
going to find this place? Not in a year, not in five years, not in
ten years. War or no war – nobody from the civilized world is
going to come down into this crater.'

Nance doesn't say anything. He hears what I'm telling him
and he knows what I mean, but he's not buying it, not just yet.
He knows where each of us is coming from – he's an enlisted
man, I'm an officer. I may not be a career man like the turkeys
from Annapolis or the Point, but I'm not like he is. He goes
back to lousy chow in the enlisted men's mess, to fifty-four
dollars a month and insults from cracker sergeants who think
all Negroes should be slaves; he knows what that's like. Here
he's an honoured guest; there he's a nigger.

Finally he gets up and strolls out of the house. I raise myself
on an elbow and watch him cross the open space that forms a
square in centre of the village. Half a dozen kids are following
him, calling 'Na! Na!' which is the version of his name they've
settled on. He bends down and sweeps up two of them, putting
one on each shoulder; then a third scrambles up on his back.
Several women are crossing to the place where a small waterfall
that tumbles down from the plain above makes a pool. The
women call to Nance and wave shyly at him; then they begin to
giggle. No, I think, Nance is no fool.

I have decided we will leave in three days. Nance is not pleased
and has not said that he will go, but I think when the time
comes he will come with me; otherwise he will be disobeying
orders, and I doubt if he is going to do that.

But we need a guide or the whole thing will be nothing more
than a shot in the dark. I have given up on the elders, who
continue to pretend that they do not understand what we want,
and have begun talking to some of the younger men in the
village. They are frightened but a few of them are more daring

than the others. And there is my watch. They look at this small metal and glass instrument as if it were magic, never tiring of watching the second hand sweep round and round. I have tried to explain what it is for but without much luck. These people consider it a magic charm, filled with a strange kind of life; in no way do they connect it with time or the telling of time. By gesture, I have shown that I will give this watch to the men who guide us out of the crater and through the mountains to the land of the Kelabit. No man has said he will do this yet, but now that they know we are leaving the watch is an object of even greater interest than before, and hourly men stop by to inspect it.

When night comes and Nance and I eat, I notice that the house where the elders meet is crowded. Men are talking, sometimes in the soft, steady tone that means one of the elders is holding forth at length, sometimes at a higher, more excited pitch. I cannot understand any of the words, but I know that the old men are not doing all the talking. This means that the young men will not readily agree to the elders' wishes. When the meeting ends and the people walk back to their houses to sleep, several of them pass our building, peering towards us as they do so. There is something melancholy in their stare.

During the night rain falls. I am wakened by the noise and sit up. Across from me I can see the hall where the elders hold council. The old men are still talking and smoking their pipes, trying to drive away with words the trouble they feel closing in. They will let us go – they are too awed by us to directly oppose our wishes – but they are not happy.

Morning comes, cool and filled with bright golden sunshine. Steam rises from the jungle as the rainfall of the night before evaporates in the already hot sunshine. We rise and eat breakfast. Today is our last day in the village, our last chance to convince someone to be our guide. The elders remain in their shelter, smoking and talking, as if they were filibustering to stop what they know is inevitable. But the rest of the people seem to have accepted our leaving. Several women stop by our building and leave food that we can take on our journey – pieces of fruit and roots and a kind of grain, almost like wild rice. Children take up a place outside our building and squat down, watching our every move. Usually there are half a dozen kids doing this, but today all the children in the village have come.

When we finish breakfast Nance takes a stroll and the children follow him, chanting his name and begging to be carried on his shoulders. I lie back and try to smoke the cigarettes I have made out of a leaf that resembles tobacco which one of the village men has given me. The smoke is acrid but the sensation of smoking relaxes me. I start to think about our trek through the jungle. It won't do any good to try to foresee the difficulties we'll meet. We'll have to keep pushing ahead, constantly checking our position against the sun. I have the map of the region imprinted on my mind and a good idea of roughly where we are. If we keep heading directly south we'll run into a tributary of the Kayan called the Balui. This branch of the Kayan cuts diagonally across our path, so that even if I have miscalculated by twenty or thirty miles we will intercept it. Then all we will have to do is follow it north-east until it forks and we will be back on the stream that leads to the land of the Kelabit. The thing is risky but not impossible. We will need guts and we will have to make certain we do not wander too far off course, but with a little luck we'll make it.

What really concerns me is what we will find when we return to the Kelabit long house. Montgomery is probably dead by now, so it is useless to worry about him. There is no telling what Johnson has done, but I can't concern myself with that either. It is the priest who I am wondering about. I'm pretty sure the Japanese who captured us were looking for him. The distance between the village where the Japs caught us and the valley of the Kelabit could not have been more than twenty-five or thirty miles; that means the Japs will have reached there long ago. There is a real possibility that by the time we arrive the priest will have either been taken away or killed and that we will be walking straight into a trap.

I am brooding on this possibility when a shadow falls across the ground immediately in front of me. I look up to see two men grinning sheepishly at me. Both are young and healthy-looking, but there is nothing particularly distinctive about them, and I assume that they are merely two more bucks who have come to look at the magic watch which they know they will never possess.

One of the men – shorter and stouter than the other with a gap between his front teeth – scratches a picture on the ground then indicates that I should look at it. It is a picture of some mountains. Then he scratches a twisting, curving line through these mountains. This must be a river. Finally he draws four small stick figures and points first to me, then off towards the far side of the square where Nance is sitting in state amidst a mob of children, then to himself and his friend. His meaning is clear: he wants to be our guide.

He grins at me sheepishly again and I follow his eyes: he and his friend are both looking at my watch. I raise my arm so that they can see it better. They stare at it in fascination. After letting them do this for a minute, I remove it and place it around the wrist of the stocky fellow. He holds it up so that his friend can watch the second hand; then I take them to the darkest place under the roof, cover the watch with a cloth and indicate that they should peek under it. The stocky fellow gives a loud exclamation of amazement: he has seen the numbers and second hand glowing in the darkness. After he and his friend have a hurried exchange, his friend bends down so that he too can peer under the cloth. For several minutes he stands like a man staring at a peep show in a penny arcade. Finally, satisfied, he raises his head and gives me a broad smile. I have my guides.

That night neither Nance nor I can sleep. We are both too keyed up and lie awake for a long time. The elders have continued their meeting, but now they are the only ones in attendance. They know that our leaving is a certainty and now their voices are a steady, dull monotone, as if they are commiserating over their loss. Nance has been very quiet. When I told him that I had found guides he said nothing. I wonder what he is feeling. He spent all afternoon with the children and after we had eaten, when their parents called them to go to their own buildings, they did not want to leave. Some even cried and had to be pulled away, crying 'Na! Na!'

Nance really loves these people. He can sit for hours listening to them babble on; he feels good just being around them and it doesn't seem to matter that he knows only a few words of their language – he communicates with them in some other way that has nothing much to do with words.

I doze off finally. When I wake it seems as if only a moment has passed, but the sun is already above the horizon and our guides are waiting, the gap-toothed fellow still wearing his grin and my watch. I collect the things I want to take with us; they make up two large packs which I cover with pieces of rough cloth made of leaves woven into a primitive sort of fabric. All this time Nance has not stirred, but now, finally, I can see him sitting with his back braced against one of the posts supporting the house, watching me work. He has a sullen, depressed look.

It takes me about fifteen minutes to complete packing. When I have finished and look up I discover that a mob of people have assembled. They have come so quietly that I hardly noticed. The whole village is standing before me, watching my movements with a single, serious, troubled expression. The crowd separates and the elders approach and one of them begins a long speech. The people look bored and some of them yawn. Children fidget and stare at me.

When the first elder has finished speaking, another follows and after him yet another. I am beginning to doubt whether we will ever start our journey. When the third man has concluded, a fourth steps to the front and comes towards me. In his hands are two necklaces made of pieces of bone. He puts one of these around my neck and then stands, watching. He is waiting for Nance, who has remained behind me in the shadows of the house, to step forward. Now is the moment – if Nance is going to stay he will not accept the necklace. It will be a simple, effective way to make his decision known: he will never have a better opportunity.

The people's eyes move to him. They look confused. A minute passes and nothing happens. Instinct is telling Nance to stay. Here, away from officers and uniforms and regulations, those things have less power. The jungle and the insects and the snakes – those are real; a man has to fear them and be wary of them. The military is thousands of miles away, in another world.

Then I see the eyes of the people move and suddenly the old man is draping the second necklace over Nance's head. Now the children look sad.

The guides come forward and hoist the packs onto their shoulders. They begin to cross the square and head towards the place under the trees where the path to the plain above begins. We follow them and behind us come the villagers, silently dogging our steps. When we reach the place where the path begins we stop for a minute and make a final farewell. The children have begun to cry and then the adults too start to weep.

'Com'on, Cap – I can't take any more of this,' says Nance, pushing past me and starting up the path almost at a trot.

XI

That first day we cover about thirty miles. The guides know this part of the country well and move quickly and confidently. We have long since passed through the valley where we were intercepted by the villagers carrying torches. We walked through it for only a short while then climbed through a notch in the hills on one side and entered another valley. I try to ask the guides how the villagers knew that we would be there when they intercepted us, but they only smile and nod. Whether they understand my question or not I don't know, but I have a feeling that they do understand and simply will not answer. The jungle is full of secrets. They spring out of its depths as suddenly as a panther and a man is too busy watching for the next surprise to think very long about the past.

When the sun sinks we bed down in a cave. It is apparent that our guides have been this far before, but I doubt if they have gone much farther. So far they have done well for us, but I can sense their growing worry. We are only four; should we encounter a party of raiders we will not have a chance. These men are not really at home in the jungle. I can tell that from the way they move. The Kelabit slide through the forest, turning aside vines and branches gently so that there is hardly a trace where they have passed. These men break branches and tear leaves, leaving an obvious track. To the stings and bites of insects the Kelabit seemed impervious, as if their skins were leather, but the insects bother these men and their arms and faces are covered with nearly as many bumps as ours.

Once inside the cave they appear to relax a little. We notice that there are signs that men have been here before – the ashes of a fire and several places where the ground is smooth and even, as if men have dug and shaped it so that they could sleep comfortably.

The guides have a discussion before they sleep. The serious tone of their voices confirms my suspicion that they are worried. They speak softly, almost in a whisper. When they have finished Nance twists towards me.

'I think they'll stay with us one more day, Captain. The stocky guy wants to go farther but his friend is worried.'

'Head hunters?' I ask.

'I think we're passing through their territory now.'

'How well do you understand what they say?' I ask.

'Well enough to know that we ought to be worried too,' he answers.

A hand on my shoulder wakens me. It is the stocky guide. He looks worried and is talking very quickly, with great excitement. I can see Nance at my shoulder, listening.

'Trouble, Captain,' he says. 'This fellow has been up already scouting around. I think he's trying to tell us there's a war party nearby.'

I can see the other guide, his eyes wide with terror. Now the two start to speak; it's clear that they are arguing.

'The short fellow wants to leave. He says we can circle around the raiders. His friend wants to stay put.'

The argument continues and I begin to collect our gear. After I've finished I beckon to the others and point towards the mouth of the cave. The two guides stop arguing and the short guy starts for the entrance, but the other draws back deeper into the shadows.

'He's scared out of his mind, Captain,' says Nance.

'I trust the other guy's judgment,' I say. 'This joker is going to get us caught.'

Nance nods and slaps the taller guide twice across the face, and the man begins to whimper. When Nance raises his hand to strike him again, he stumbles towards the mouth of the cave.

We move quickly now, at a jog that sometimes turns into a trot. The short guy is in the lead. I can see the sweat beading on the back of his neck. Right behind him comes his friend, who keeps peering from side to side, trying to see into the jungle, as if he expected the raiders to leap out at any minute.

We follow a narrow stream for a quarter mile until it enters a swamp. Here we must go more slowly, gingerly feeling our way to avoid quicksand; then we are on solid ground again, moving quickly down a wide, sun-lit valley through which runs a strongly-flowing river, glinting silver in the early morning sunlight. The guides start to run and we have to struggle to keep up. Both of them continually twist their heads and peer over their shoulders, as if they've heard something Nance and I have missed. Nance looks back too then tells me to move faster.

I pick up the pace and move up beside the two guides who are now struggling with our packs on their shoulders. Ahead the floor of the valley rises then drops out of sight. The vegetation is thinner here, and anybody closing in from behind will be able to spot us easily at the top of the rise where there are no trees, only tall grass and the bare banks of the river.

Then we are climbing the last fifty yards to the summit, scrambling up loose, treacherous rock that gives way as we go, sending pebbles flying down the incline. At the summit trees begin again and we move into them. Then Nance stops and peers back down the valley.

'There!' he says, pointing into the distance.

I see nothing at first; then they come into view. At this distance they are hardly more then tiny dots moving against the green background. They would not be visible except for the white paint covering their faces.

The guides stand beside Nance, staring at the oncoming figures. The short guy's expression is grim; his friend is terrified.

'We've got to move fast,' says Nance. 'We've got twenty minutes, maybe a half hour on them – not more.'

We continue moving parallel to the river for a few hundred yard; then, abruptly, the guides turn to the right and head into the forest. The move is a gamble; the going is slower in the forest so that if the raiders are following us they will gain ground. But if they are merely passing through the valley they will continue on past us and we will be safe.

It is dark because the foliage of the roof of the forest is thick letting only an occasional ray of light penetrate through. The forest floor is covered with ferns and vines and the trunks of the trees are sometimes so close together that we have to weave our way between them. It seems inconceivable that anyone could follow our trail in this labyrinth.

Finally we halt, exhausted, sweat pouring from us. A cloud of mosquitoes hovers around our heads. The guides are arguing again, their voices harsh whispers as they gasp for breath. Nance is breathing deeply but he still seems fresh and strong. I can tell that he is listening to the guides.

'Nobody will find us in here,' I say. 'We don't have to push so hard.'

He gives me a glum nod.

'These guys don't know where we are, Captain – we're lost and we may even be going in circles.'

'Why don't we just wait here?' I say. 'If we give the raiders an hour or two they will be so far ahead of us that we won't have to worry; then we can continue along the valley.'

Nance shakes his head. 'If they were following us and they don't catch up they will know that something is fishy and they'll come back or maybe set up an ambush.'

'And if they weren't?'

'Can we take that chance, Captain?'

'We can't go on this way. Not even natives can travel cross-country through the jungle in Borneo. The only other option is to go back to the valley and backtrack.'

'I don't know, Captain – it doesn't feel good to me. I got a feeling that we should keep on going the way we are.'

I know I'm right – if we keep on it's hopeless – but I don't think I'll be able to convince the guides. They're worried about their own skins now and they'll keep running. Already I can see that they want to be off, pushing deeper into this pathless forest where we cannot even see the sun to guide ourselves.

The short fellow suddenly drops to his knees and puts his ear to the ground. I watch the tense play of his features. Quickly he leaps to his feet and points in a direction to the right, and we start off, moving as fast as we can. Now both guides rush forward headlong, tripping over roots and vines, sometimes colliding with tree trunks. Nance and I try to follow them but gradually they are getting ahead of us. The forest seems to grow darker, the foliage overhead thicker. From the branches dangle vines, so numerous that they form a curtain that we must continually push aside. The floor of the forest is covered with thick moss, and now and then we see great clumps of tropical violets and sometimes orchids.

We can see the guides no longer now and must move on sheer instinct, hoping that we are not circling back on our tracks. Nance stays beside me, and if one of us forges ahead he slows down until the other has caught up. Suddenly Nance freezes and drops to the ground, pulling me down beside him. He twists his head and looks behind us and finally puts his ear to the ground. I do the same and at first hear nothing; then I am aware of a tremor, as if a herd of horses were galloping. That can mean only one thing – many men are coming, moving very fast. Even as I listen the vibration intensifies.

Nance springs to his feet and grabs the closest vine and gives it a yank. It holds firm and suddenly he is off the ground, going upward, hand over hand, as fast as he can. I grab a vine and start to climb, but it begins to give and I reach out before my feet strike the ground, grabbing another. This one holds.

I am not as strong as Nance and have to use my feet to climb, but fear gives me energy I never knew I had. We climb up and up – thirty, forty, fifty feet. Still we have not reached the safety of the branches and foliage of the forest's roof. Nance is almost thirty feet above me and still climbing. My vine begins to swing and I tighten my grip and look down and suddenly I am almost overcome with dizziness. I shut my eyes and hold on grimly, twine my legs around the vine, and try to bring the panic that is sweeping through me under control. Finally I open my eyes again, making certain that I do not look down this time. Nance is so far above that he looks like a midget. I start to climb again, slower this time, hand over hand. I am making steady progress now, but I have to rest every twenty feet or so. Now I can see Nance more clearly. He is lying on a branch, peering towards me. He seems to be beckoning me on; then suddenly he holds his hands out to me, spreading his fingers. It takes a moment for me to realise that he is telling me to stop.

I twine my feet around the vine and wait, peering down. This time I do not get dizzy. A minute passes and then I see a man. He seems to glide between the trees, he stops and drops to the ground to listen, then moves on. He is moving on a path parallel to the one we travelled on but about twenty feet to the right. Were it not for that twenty feet he would surely have spotted our tracks.

Now Nance is beckoning me and I begin to climb again. I move faster now, my strength seeming to increase with each foot I ascend. I can see Nance clearly now. He is wrapped around a stout branch and above him is a thick roof of living green, glowing warmly because of the sunlight above it.

The final part of the climb is hard. My strength is nearly

spent, but I am so close that it is only a matter of a few feet until I am on the branch, stretched flat and panting like a winded hound-dog. Nance slides forward and hauls up the vines that we climbed. When he has lifted both vines and tied them around the branch, he points upwards and vanishes into the leaves. A second later I follow him.

It is amazingly warm in the leaves, and they are filled with buzzing flies. Immediately beneath us there is a small opening that lets us see the floor of the forest far below. We wait and watch. An hour passes, then another. The afternoon wears on and the heat increases. Nance removes his belt and circles my chest under the arms and then the branch with it, knotting it tightly. I do the same with my own belt at the waist. I will sleep while he keeps watch; then we will change places. I close my eyes and almost immediately drop off, my ears filled with the droning of a million hungry flies.

Nance is whispering in my ear to be quiet. I am still groggy and it takes a minute for the meaning of his words to register. Through the chink in the leaves I can barely see the forest floor below. It is covered with shadow, with here and there a tiny patch of light, that from this great height gives it a peculiar, speckled look. Suddenly I see a figure, tiny with distance, pass through one of the illuminated spots. As my eyes become accustomed to the shadows I make out more and more figures. They are moving slowly. From this great height it is difficult to see them clearly, but it looks as if they are searching the forest floor for tracks. A man is highlighted in a patch of sunlight, and I can see the white paint that covers his face. He is staring up into the roof of the forest. Then there is a cry and the figures move to one spot and form a circle. Now they all stare up.

The voices of the raiders rise to us. There is a calm about the sound that is unnerving, as if they were discussing the weather or the best place in a stream to fish rather than how to find two men to slaughter.

'They will have to reach us first,' Nance whispers. 'That won't be so easy.'

The raiders hold a council; then they all lift their bows and the air is filled with arrows. They slice through the leaves and two stick fast in the underside of the branch that we are sitting on. But none hit us.

They fire three volleys then stop and five men choose vines and begin to ascend, moving with amazing rapidity. By now they must have guessed that we have pulled up the vines we used; that means they plan to crawl through the branches until they find us. The place where our tracks abruptly end is crystal clear, so it will be easy for them to surround us then crawl towards the centre until they make contact. We watch them climb until they disappear into the leaves; then there is nothing to do except wait. At least we have the machetes that the villagers gave us, so we'll have the satisfaction of getting a few of them before they overwhelm us.

Nance remains absolutely still, listening not only with his ears but with his whole body. His eyes narrow and the muscles in his jaw tense. The silence is absolute except for the buzz of the flies. Then I can see the white face and hands of the raider. He is about thirty feet away, farther out on the branch where it begins to divide and thin. How he got there I don't know, probably crossed from the branch of a nearby tree, for the roof of this forest is like one great leafy carpet. He is advancing towards us slowly, wrapped around the branch like a snake. Why he doesn't call out to his comrades I can't tell; perhaps he thinks we have not seen him and does not want to give himself away.

Nance turns to me and whispers that I should hold tight; then, in one smooth, lightning-quick motion, he springs upwards until he grasps the branch above and hangs from it, resting his feet on the branch I'm sitting on. He pushes the branch with his feet again and again, building up a rhythm that makes the arc through which the branch swings grow wider and wider. If I were not strapped to the branch with two belts, I would be thrown off, but the man crawling towards us has nothing to hold fast with except his hands. I watch in fascination as he struggles to maintain his grip. He is strong, a good climber, but the branch is swinging wildly, and at the end – where he is – the arc is almost twenty feet. Several times he is flung off but retains his grip and manages to scramble back.

Nance increases the speed of the swings and alternates the rhythm – two vigorous swings then a gentle one then two more hard ones. The man falls, catching the branch with one hand. Nance pushes the branch faster, and the raider loses his grip, screaming as he falls. Now others will come, for they cannot have failed to spot us.

Two more men try to reach us and each time Nance manages to dislodge them. A third man stays at a distance shooting arrows, but the branches and leaves are so thick that these will never reach us.

The afternoon has almost ended. Already the sun is sinking and darkness is coming to the forest. For a few moments, the glow from the sun still throws an eerie half light on the forest floor below; then everything is black.

We lie in the darkness and wait. The sounds of the forest seem weirdly clear, amplified. A bird is chirping; then we hear it pecking the bark of a nearby branch, probably in search of a meal. Mosquitoes buzz around us. The flies are still droning and now, with the coming of darkness, other insects join the chorus.

'You think they'll try something in the dark, Captain?' Nance asks.

'I don't know,' I say. 'If they're like the Kelabit, they won't want to stay in the forest at night. They might go and come back in the morning; that would give us a chance to make a break for it.'

'We'd leave tracks,' Nance says. 'And they move a lot faster in the forest than we do. They would catch us easy.'

'We have to do something,' I say. 'We can't just sit here waiting for God to help us.'

Nance gives a low laugh.

'Seems I heard that before, Captain – seems that was pretty much what you said before we left the crater.'

The night drags on but nothing happens. We peer into the forest, looking for the glimmer of a fire that will mean the raiders have stayed. There is only darkness.

'They've gone,' I say. 'They're terrified of the dark – all these people are. If they had stayed they would have built a fire.'

Nance is not convinced.

'We should at least try to make a break for it,' I say. 'When it starts to get light we just go up again – there are vines everywhere. If we keep moving, sooner or later something will break our way. You gotta have faith, Nance – you gotta believe. We don't know what will happen down there, but at least if we try something we have a chance; otherwise all they have to do is wait and starve us out.'

Nance doesn't answer. He's been pushed to the wall and has

made up his mind that this is where he'll make his stand. It's a question of inertia – he's done all the moving he intends to. He's not acting terrified, although he has to be as worried as I am. Instead he's just acting stupid, and the more frightened he becomes the stupider he'll act. There is only one thing left to do and I decide to do it.

'I'm going down, Nance,' I say. 'You can stay here or you can come along. That's your decision.'

I move out along the branch, feeling for one of the vines that he drew up and knotted. I'm clumsy up here and I've always been terrified of heights, but now is not the time to think about that. I find the vine, untie it, and drop it into space; then I move down into the darkness, hand over hand, my legs twisted around the vine to slow my descent. I am mortally afraid – the old fear of heights is sweeping over me again – but in a vague way I realize this is good: if I wasn't so frightened of falling I would be thinking about what might happen when I reach the ground.

I come to the end of the vine and reach out with my feet – nothing. There is no way of knowing how far beneath me the ground is. Perhaps part of the vine broke off; maybe I did not unwind it all. If I drop I may break an ankle, but I've come this far and all I can do is complete things. I lower myself until my arms are fully extended then let go.

I land lightly on all fours, like a cat. The drop was only a few feet, but if the raiders are there, waiting, they will have heard me.

Nothing happens. I twist my head and whistle softly so that Nance can hear me: there is no response. I try again, this time whistling 'reveille'. My whistle is echoed back from above, then the vine begins to jump and tremble as Nance descends.

It takes him half as long as it took me but we move off quickly, heading due west, hoping the raiders have chosen another direction.

We cannot move too quickly because of the darkness and we bump into trees continually, so that we have to feel our way like blind men. The insects are ferocious and it is stiflingly hot. Up above, there was at least the semblance of a breeze, but down here the air is absolutely still. We know we are leaving a trail that can be followed but we have no choice. When dawn comes we will still have a short time when we can be relatively sure that we will not be overtaken; then perhaps we can change tactics so that we leave a more obscure trail.

Suddenly I freeze, and Nance, sensing I've stopped, halts too.

Off to the right at a distance of about twenty yards I can see two glowing yellow spots.

'That's been following us for a half hour, Captain,' Nance says.

'What is it?' I ask.

'Maybe a leopard,' he says.

We begin moving again and the spots move too; they glide smoothly, never hurried, and always they are there, never farther away, never closer. The effect is unnerving. I want to draw my machete to defend myself in case it charges, but I need both hands free to feel my way between the tree trunks.

Gradually the darkness grows less intense. First we see the trunks of trees, then each other, as we slog along. I look for the two yellow spots – they have gone.

We continue for two hours then I tell Nance to stop.

'We better go up again,' I say. 'They'll be coming if they are going to come and it'll be soon.'

It takes fifteen more minutes to find a vine. This time we find one hanging all alone, not another within sight – here we will be nearly invulnerable. The place is at the bottom of a long, gentle decline that runs for almost half a mile. Around it the ground is thick with ferns and so soft that it is almost swamp. The roof of the forest is enormously high here – easily two hundred feet – and the trees are old with great thick trunks that have almost no branches until they have risen over one hundred feet. It is ideal.

Nance wants me to go first, but I am too winded. He starts up; the distance is enormous and it takes him a long time. I begin to grow uneasy but do not want to start climbing until he has finished. We have tested the vine and it seems strong, but there is no telling for certain whether it can bear two men.

Nance reaches the top and signals to me and I start up. This vine is different from the one I climbed yesterday: smoother and harder to grasp. For every two or three feet I gain I lose one.

After having ascended only thirty feet I am sweating and winded and have to stop to rest. I am much weaker than I realized; I don't know if I'll be able to make it.

'They're coming!' yells Nance. 'Climb, Captain! climb like a bastard!'

I begin again, working frantically. I can see them beneath the trees at the very top of the rise. They have seen me and they are running now, shouting as they come. At most, I have two or three minutes.

Hand over hand I go, almost like a machine: ten feet, twenty feet – I no longer feel fatigue or the pain in my hands, only a cold, all-enveloping terror.

When they reach the vine I am a hundred feet up. They stand for a minute, as if uncertain how to proceed; then a man leaps on the vine and starts up after me.

'Don't stop!' yells Nance. 'Keep coming! keep coming!'

My strength is gone: I move upwards but my speed diminishes and below me the raider is gaining fast. I try to summon all my remaining strength but it does no good. I have pushed myself too much already – adrenalin can carry a man only so far. I get dizzy, things go out of focus. Then Nance's voice calls me back to myself.

'Cut it!' he yells. 'Cut the vine!'

The raider is now only about thirty feet below. I can see his face clearly. His eyes are cold and hard, as if he is calculating the best way to take me.

I clamp my feet around the vine and begin to saw with my machete. The outer crust is hard, but once I have broken through this and penetrated the green pulp it goes fast. It is difficult holding myself in place and working the machete at the same time, because I can't get much leverage.

A hand seizes my ankle and I have to grab the vine with both hands or plummet down. My machete falls; I am defenceless, a hundred feet above the jungle floor. I kick viciously with my free foot and strike the man in the jaw. He looses his grip on my ankle and grabs onto the vine, sliding down a few feet.

Miraculously, he has held on to his knife, and now he starts to ascend again, creeping towards me, the knife between his teeth.

Without warning the vine tears.

He is gone and I find myself dangling in space, my grip a few scant inches above the stub end of the vine.

I pull myself up an inch at a time. My arms are wracked with pain, my hands feel numb and clumsy. If I can only move up far enough to clasp the vine with my knees and feet I will be all right; then I will be able to rest and regain my strength. But my hands seem frozen; they no longer obey my will.

'Pull, Captain! pull!' Nance yells.

I can see the raiders below me, waiting, their white faces

hideous masks in the early morning shadows that cover the forest floor.

With a last supreme effort I will my hands to move: first one then the other. I am doing it – somewhere I am finding the strength. And then I have moved high enough to wrap my legs around the vine and am breathing heavily, my eyes closed in sheer exhaustion, waiting for the second wind that will take me on to the top.

Why the raiders do not shoot me with their arrows, I do not know. Possibly, they used them all yesterday. A few try to use blowguns, but the distance is too great. I climb steadily until I can see Nance smiling, waiting with outstretched hands.

Then I am on the branch, a perch like an eagle's, so far above the forest floor that the raiders, waiting below in frustration, look like miniature make-believe figures.

'Rest!' says Nance, as he drapes me over a branch and ties me fast with my belt. 'Rest now 'cause pretty soon you're gonna need all the energy you got.'

I wake coughing. The raiders have built a fire and the air is thick with smoke. We watch them adding more fallen branches to the fire burning at the bottom of the tree. Nance chuckles.

'It'll never burn, Captain – they're wasting their time.'

He's right. They keep trying for almost an hour but the tree will not catch fire. Everything is saturated with water, so that in the end the only effect of all their work is to make clouds of thick grey smoke.

The few vines in this part of the forest belong to trees far away from ours, and although some men climb up to try to cross to us they soon give up, for the distance is great and the branches meet where they are thin and weak, at a considerable distance from the tree trunks.

The day wanes, night begins to fall, and we watch as the raiders retire back up the hill they ran down, disappearing into the shadows of the forest.

This night is as black as the last. Again we scan the forest for signs of a camp fire but see nothing.

We are both dizzy and lightheaded from lack of nourishment. The raiders can't reach us here, but if they wait long enough we will have to come down – either that or strap ourselves to our perch and starve where we are.

'We've got to find food,' I say. 'We can't last much longer without it.'

'How are we going to get down?' Nance asks. 'There's at least a hundred feet between the end of the vine and the ground.'

'We'll have to cross through the branches to a place where there is another vine,' I say.

Nance gives a low chuckle.

'Not me, Captain – the guys with the white faces wouldn't try it, and they could see what they were doing. Maybe if we study the branches in the day we could make a plan, but it's still a long shot. Tonight it wouldn't even be that – I ain't gonna try it.'

'Every hour we get weaker,' I say. 'We have to eat.'

'Try leaves,' Nance says. 'We got plenty of leaves, Captain.'

I have read survival manuals about what happens to people who eat leaves or grass. They get cramps and colic, worse off than if they ate nothing. We can't risk it. The only alternative is insects – there are plenty of those – but I can't bring myself to do it. Grubs yes, even though the idea nauseates me, but not insects.

Time passes and I drowse, wake, doze off again, then wake for good. Hunger is twisting my stomach into knots. To distract myself I listen to the sounds of the forest. Tonight there is something new: a peculiar rasping sound that rises then falls into silence then rises again. It is difficult to tell where it is coming from. At one point it seems to be ahead of us, in a part of the forest we have not reached yet; then it circles behind us, at the top of the long decline; then we hear it on the other side.

I ask Nance what he thinks it is.

'The thing with the yellow eyes,' he answers.

'Leopards can climb trees, can't they?' I say. Nance chuckles. 'That wasn't a joke,' I say. 'It sounds like it's hungry.'

'You wanted something to eat, Captain,' he says, chuckling again. 'Maybe this will be your chance.'

But the sound comes no closer, and then it stops and the only noise is the hum of insects. The hunger pains in my stomach are almost unbearable. To try and blunt them I press myself against the branch as hard as I can. Eventually I doze off, and for the next few hours I am in that twilight zone, drifting in and out of sleep.

A strange sensation – something eerie from a place deep inside my head – snaps me into wakefulness.

There is a new sound, as if a hard, ragged-edged object is being dragged over concrete. The sound comes from the bottom of our tree. By crawling forward several feet and parting the leaves, I have an unobstructed view of the forest floor.

At first I see nothing; then whatever is down there moves and I see two yellow dots. The thing down there has lifted its head and is peering upwards, towards the place where I am perched. Probably it heard the noise I made crawling farther out on the branch.

The eyes glow like golden fires in the darkness; then they disappear and the scratching begins again, this time louder, as if the animal were striking its claws violently against the tree. Now I hear the other sound too – a low, throaty cough that runs on and on, like a cat's purr amplified a hundred times.

'It's down there,' I say. 'Nance – do you hear me? The damn thing is at the bottom of the tree and it's trying to get up here!'

There is no answer.

'Nance!' I call. 'Nance, wake up!'

Still no answer. Nance has gone.

Slowly, I inch backwards towards the place where we were both resting. I call again, but the only answer is the hum of the insects and a rasping cough from that thing below.

Nance was too careful to roll off the branch. He had a belt – he would have been a fool not to tie it around the branch before he dozed off. But there is no other explanation. Why didn't I hear him cry out? – surely he would have cried out as he fell.

I press myself tight to the branch and try to keep cool. There must be some explanation, some reason. If I can just keep calm I'll be able to pull things together. I hear the scraping noise again, but now it is much louder.

Then there's a whistle. It is soft, barely discernible above the humming insects, and for a moment I think I must be mistaken. But there it is again, this time carrying a tune – reveille.

Nance is out there somewhere.

I return the whistle. I cannot see where he is nor understand why he has gone, but it is enough at least to know that he is still alive.

I am sweating bullets. Nance is behind me, urging me on. If I stop he tells me to keep going. I do what he tells me to do, but the sweat is dripping off me and each second, every foot that I go, I expect to topple into space and fall to my death.

We are at the very top of the tree, in the roof of the forest. Nance has found a place where we can cross to a different tree with another vine reaching almost to the forest floor. There are only two catches: the distance is almost a hundred feet, and it is pitch black so we have to feel our way. It has taken us almost an hour to go fifty feet. That means we are probably at the place where the supporting branches are at their thinnest – the place where the actual intersection occurs. Beneath us there is still a thick carpet of leaves, but should we slip there will be no reprieve.

'The spot is just a little bit ahead, Captain – about twenty feet.'

'I hope you're right,' I say. 'I'm not much good at playing monkey.'

'Move closer now. Feel with your hands. You'll find another branch crossing the one we're on. That's the one to take.'

I can feel myself trembling. 'You better be right, Nance,' I say. 'You fucking better be right.'

I move ahead cautiously, sliding along the branch, my arms on the top of it so that it supports my weight. Two times we have had to reverse this position, moving upside-down like sloths. The sensation was terrifying and I don't want to repeat it.

I feel another branch. It intersects the one we're on so it must be the branch Nance is talking about. I reach over and test it with one hand – it is thin, frighteningly thin.

'Nance,' I say. 'You gotta be kidding. This branch is a damn twig. I got the wrong one, huh?'

'That's it, Captain,' he says. He's right behind me now, so close that I can hear his breathing.

'That branch won't hold us,' I say.

'There's a lot of spring in this wood, Captain – it's a lot stronger than it looks.'

'You're crazy, Nance,' I say. 'You're out of your fucking mind.'

'You said yourself we don't have any choice, Captain – we can't stay up here without eating, and in another day our strength will be so gone that we'll never get down. We gotta try this.'

I curse; then, after taking half a dozen deep breaths to calm myself, move over onto the new branch.

It dips and I panic and hold tight; then I hear it strike the branch below, the one I just left. The two branches rub together, making a grating, creaking noise, but it doesn't dip any farther: the other branch is bracing it.

I inch ahead. I can feel the branch bow beneath me. The bend must be almost twenty-five degrees. There are numerous smaller branches budding off the main branch, and I use these to keep my balance. Slowly I ease forward, each moment expecting the branch to give way.

With a sliding, ripping sound the branch suddenly swings down. I grab frantically and hold on. It will break! I know it will break and that will be it! Trembling, I wait, listening for the crack that will mean the end.

'Climb up slow, Captain!'

It is Nance, speaking from somewhere above me.

'Go easy and you'll make it – don't panic!'

Slowly I pull myself up. The branch is leafy and I must force my way through thick foliage. Something crawls over my face – a spider? a centipede? I can feel it crossing my cheek and dropping to my neck, then down into my shirt.

Gradually the angle decreases and I notice that the branch is thickening. I go on – ten feet, fifteen feet, twenty feet. Now the branch is almost horizontal, and I am crawling on it. I've made it!

I work my way forward until I reach a major fork then stop to rest. I feel strangely empty and calm. Behind me now I can hear Nance coming on, pushing his way through the leaves; then he has reached me, and we both stop to gather our strength. I've lost my sense of time, but it seems like hours since we started to climb up towards the roof of the forest.

'We can't wait here, Captain,' Nance says. 'We got to go all the way tonight.'

'You're crazy,' I say.

'We're near the vine now. We can make it.'

'Pull it up, Nance,' I say. 'Pull it up and knot it over the branch so the raiders can't climb up. We can go down tomorrow when we're fresher. I don't have any strength left. I'll never be able to go down two hundred feet on a vine tonight, then hike far enough so that we have time to find food before we have to get back up. They'll catch us on the ground.'

'Like you said, Captain, tomorrow we'll be even weaker.'

'Unless we eat something.'

'You got any ideas how we're going to do that, Captain?

What are you going to do, order a monkey to climb over here so that we can kill it?'

'The place is full of bugs, Nance – they're climbing all over us. Bugs are protein.'

'You gotta be kiddin', Captain. Leaves, maybe, but not bugs.'

'No, Nance,' I say, reaching into my shirt and lifting out a wriggling caterpillar. 'Bugs!'

At first we both feel nauseous but eventually this passes. The secret is to avoid smelling them. Nobody ever thinks much of how bugs smell, but when they are bitten into there is a definite odour. Mostly we stay with the caterpillars. There are a million of them and they're juicy and plump. We try moths but these have a really strong odour, and even though they look like they should be easier to eat, they aren't.

Some of our strength returns. No longer are we so light-headed, and the cold sweat and chills that were racking us lessen. We doze on and off, and when morning comes we feel rested. We are thirsty but with the coming of the morning sunlight and the rapid heating of the air, the foliage, cooled during the night, is covered with beads of moisture which we lick. We are still thirsty, but at least we have found enough water to prevent dehydration.

Almost as soon as the sun has appeared over the horizon the raiders return. They go straight to the tree with the charred trunk and peer upward. Their voices rise in a buzz of excitement: they cannot see us. They spread out and begin to move from tree to tree. It takes them nearly half an hour, but finally they stop at a place almost directly beneath us. How they know where we are is a mystery, for there is no sign on the ground and we are hidden deep in the foliage two hundred feet above them.

They remain underneath us for an hour then leave, retreating back up the slope and into the shadows of the forest. We are mystified because there are still several hours of daylight left.

'We better not go down yet, Captain,' Nance says. 'I don't trust this.'

'Neither do I,' I say. 'They're probably watching this spot right now.'

When twilight comes the raiders have still not returned. Night falls and we get ready to descend the vine. I am uneasy, but we have made our plan and will stick to it.

'I don't like it, Captain,' Nance says. 'Something's not right.'

'You want to spend another night eating bugs?' I ask.

Nance lowers the vine and we descend, hand over hand, stopping every twenty feet to listen. Except for the hum of the insects there is silence. Once or twice I think I hear a rasping purr, but I do not trust my ears. Whatever those yellow eyes belonged to has been gone for a whole day; it's unlikely that it will return now. Probably it is as afraid of us as we are of it.

We reach the ground and start off, moving as quickly as we can in the darkness. We have not gone more than a hundred yards when we realize our mistake. From somewhere back up the long, sloping decline comes a soft hoot. If we hadn't spent time with the Kelabit we would think it was a bird calling in the darkness. But we know that it is not.

I start to run and Nance grabs me. 'Wait, Captain!' he says.

I stop, sweating with fear.

More hoots sound. First from the left, then the right, then straight ahead: they have us surrounded.

'Let's go back up!' I say. 'We can make it.'

'That's what they think we'll do,' Nance says. 'They probably have someone on that vine already.'

I remember that they seemed to know our exact position even though they couldn't see us in the foliage. It would be easy for them to find the vine.

'This way!' Nance says abruptly, changing direction and heading straight up the decline.

At first I think he's crazy, but then I realize that up the decline is best – the raiders will not expect us to backtrack.

We circle away from the vine, passing it at a distance of about a hundred feet. I stare towards it, trying to see if they have reached it already, but the darkness is so complete that I can't see anything.

Silently, we slip in among the trees at the top of the decline, staying low, gliding from trunk to trunk. Visibility is absolute zero: we should be all right unless we run straight into them.

The hoots come again, now not more than twenty-five yards away and straight ahead of us. Whoever is giving the call is moving towards us. We crouch down behind two trees. Next we hear the sound of footsteps and men breathing heavily. We can't be certain how many there are, but even three or four will be more than a match for us in our weakened condition.

They seem to be trotting, intent on reaching the bottom of the decline as quickly as possible. They sweep past us, so close that one man brushes against the tree I am crouching behind. We wait until we can hear them rushing down the hill then rise and move ahead. I want to run but that will be futile; I'll merely crash into a tree trunk and stun myself.

Every fifty yards we stop to orient ourselves and make sure that we are moving in a straight line, not circling. We cannot see the sky so we have to depend on instinct alone. Our progress seems painfully slow, and always – every moment – we expect to hear the sound of men behind us.

'It can't be too much farther,' Nance says. 'We should reach the valley and the river any minute now.'

Then we hear it – a soft hoot somewhere behind us, echoed softly a minute later from another place to our right.

We go faster, crashing ahead, barging into trees, careening from one trunk to the next. The calls sound again, this time closer. They hear us now and are closing in. Then I hear a new sound: a coughing, rasping purr – the leopard is somewhere out there, somewhere close at hand. The raiders must hear the new sound and surely they know what is making it, but it has no effect on them; their calls continue, coming closer and closer.

Suddenly I stop dead. The two yellow dots are straight ahead of us, not thirty feet away. The purring sound comes again, low and throaty. Nance has heard it and now he stops too. Behind us the hoots are getting louder and louder. We hear voices and the tramp of feet.

'Get down!' says Nance. We crouch. The voices grow louder, and as they do the purr increases in volume. Now the raiders cannot be more than twenty or thirty yards behind us. Suddenly the purr breaks into a growl and the two dots move, at first a step or two, then in a great whirring bound directly towards us. I raise my hands but it sweeps past us. We can hear it crashing through the undergrowth; then there is a scream like no scream I have ever heard before. The purr is high-pitched now, and mixed with it are human cries.

'Let's get out of here!' Nance says.

We bang into tree trunks, fall, struggle to our feet and plunge ahead. Soon the trees start thinning out; there is more space between them and we can move faster. Then the trees are behind us and in front of us lies the floor of the valley, with the river gleaming in the moonlight. We stop. We can go left, back to the crater and the gentle people we have left behind, or right, towards the land of the Kelabit.

I see Nance looking towards me. He knows what he wants to do, but he is waiting for me to decide. I shake my head.

'We'll be no better off back there than we were before we started.'

We turn right and climb to the top of the grade. At the summit we pause. Before us lies a vast, rolling forest, the river twisting through it like a great silver snake. I remember the map the guides drew in the dust back in the crater: we are on the right path.

Nance is looking back, far down the valley towards the tree-covered hills behind us.

'Com'on,' I say. 'We better make time.'

We move ahead at a brisk walk and then break into a trot. We are both half-starved, bruised and covered from head to toe with scratches and insect bites, but we feel fresh. .By morning we will have covered enough territory so that the raiding party will never catch up with us.

XII

For two days and a night we follow the river as it twists and turns through the tree-covered hills. Just after nightfall of the second day it divides, one branch turning north, the other and larger branch rushing off to the south-east. According to our calculations, we have been heading almost due south, which should have taken us beyond the Kelabit country; the branch that heads north should lead us back into the heart of that territory.

All night we follow the northern branch, but just after dawn we pause. We are above a great, cascading rapids which descends sharply for nearly half a mile. Beyond this, the river makes a giant curve back on itself, ultimately heading almost due west. If we follow it we will be returning to the land we passed through – the country of the raiders.

'We've got to go back,' I say. 'We have to try the other branch of the river.'

Nance is sitting. He is worn and tired and disgusted.

'How do you know that branch will be any better than this one, Captain?'

I can't answer him because I'm going on instinct, and there's no way to prove instinct.

'Rest up a few minutes,' I say. 'Then we'll start back. It's light now – we'll be able to make better time.'

'So will they,' he says.

'They?'

'The guys with the white faces. I figure we got about six or seven hours on them, not more. That's the difference in time between when the leopard attacked and dawn. By then they would have regrouped and started tracking us.'

'They wouldn't come this far, Nance – this isn't their turf. These people stay within the boundaries of their tribal territory.'

'You might have read that in a book, Captain, but I'm not sure those guys read the same book.'

'Ten minutes, Nance,' I say. 'Save your breath – we'll need it to make time.'

He's near breaking point. If we don't reach the land of the Kelabit soon, trouble will start. Two men tugging different ways in a trackless jungle will never make it.

By noon we have reached the fork in the river and started up the other branch. I look for signs of the raiders, half afraid that we will be walking into them. My reason tells me this is nonsense – I have decided on a plan and the thing to do is carry it through – but I have been in the jungle too long and everything seems to be slipping away, except fear.

We walk until sundown then rest for an hour. The river is still heading south-west, leading us farther and farther from the Kelabit country, but we have no choice except to follow it.

Toward midnight the terrain becomes rougher and we pass two rapids. Here, the going is hard and we slip and slide over sharp rocks, bruising our feet. The boots that we have worn since we put ashore outside Tanjungselor are now rotten and soft, torn in many places; they will not last much longer. Clouds cover the moon so that our vision is limited to the river and the nearby jungle. For a long time now the river has been corkscrewing, so that we are uncertain of the direction it is heading in. The terrain seems to be made up of an endless series of rolling forested hills, with the river snaking between them. Nance says we are descending but I haven't been aware of this.

When the sun rises we discover that we are heading due south and my heart sinks. At this rate we will miss the Kelabit country completely and end up in the trackless swamps above Banjarmasin. That city is a Jap stronghold, and all of the land to its north for hundreds of miles is impenetrable mangrove swamp, rife with malaria and yellow fever. If we stumble into that swamp our chances of getting out alive are zero. I wonder if Nance realizes this.

Now we pause because there is a new sound. We have been travelling in the jungle for so long that we have become like animals, our senses of smell and hearing honed to razor-sharpness. The sound is distant but to us unmistakable: an unending roar that can be caused by only one thing – rapids.

We move on doggedly for two hours as the river zigs and zags before we come to them. The sight is awesome. The river is almost straight here, descending at an angle of thirty-five degrees for at least a mile. All the way it seems to be boiling white foam. The air is filled with a fine mist and three small rainbows span the river, like miniature bridges, halfway down the gradient.

Slowly we labour down the incline. The rocks along the river-bank are slippery. We fall several times, cutting our hands and knees. The mist soaks our clothes.

It takes us over an hour to reach the great tree-covered bluff at the bottom of the hill. Here we rest for a half hour, lying in the sunshine to dry ourselves. I doze off for what seems like a few minutes, but when I wake I am bathed in sweat and my face is burned raw.

I scramble to my feet, but Nance is not in sight. I hear a shout and he appears, running towards me along the river-bank where it borders the bluff. He stops when he is still a hundred feet away and beckons me to follow, then turns and heads back around the bluff. I run after him.

Beyond the bluff the river broadens and is joined by a tributary before it turns eastward. Something about the place gives me an odd feeling; then I realize the reason – we have been here before, but the last time we came up the river from the east. And the tributary, the stream flowing gently from the south-west, led us to the land of the Kelabit.

XIII

We enter the village of the Kelabit at midday, passing women who are bathing and children playing. They look at us but say nothing. The village seems the same, but we notice that many of the men are absent – probably off on a hunting expedition. As we pass under the entrance arch we look up, trying to see if more heads have been hung there since we left.

Our rooms are still empty and the pallets we slept on remain. We are both hungry and tired. Nance tells some of the children that we need food and this is brought.

We eat then fall into a deep sleep that lasts for a whole day. When we waken it is morning and we go outside, stretch, then stroll to the pond which the men use for bathing.

Half a dozen boys are there, swimming and paddling in circles. They laugh and scream when they see Nance, and he splashes them.

We swim around for a while and then come out. While I lie in the sun, drying myself, Nance hold a rudimentary conversation with his friends. The sun is high overhead now and, even though I have shut my eyes, I can still see it, a fiery ball burning in the darkness. I roll over onto my stomach.

'The Japs have been here, Captain,' Nance says matter-of-factly.

I sit up.

'They came almost a month ago, only five days after we left.'

I calculate – that would have been shortly after we escaped from them.

'How do you know this?' I ask.

106

'The kids. One of them is missing and I asked where he was. They said he was killed – when the Japs busted in they riddled the long house with machine-gun fire.'

'And the priest?'

'He got away into the jungle. He's back now. The people have sentries stationed on the river. If the Japs come back they'll try to give a warning so the Kelabit will have enough time to hide in the jungle.'

'What about Johnson and Montgomery and the Malay?'

'Montgomery never came back. The Malay's OK and Johnson's still here. The kids say Johnson's acting crazy. The Jap attack shook him up.'

After lunch I go to talk with the priest. He is sitting alone in the cool shadows of his room. When I rap on the post outside his doorway he tells me to enter, using English so that I know he was expecting me.

'You were gone a long time,' he says. 'We thought that the jungle had eaten you.'

'It tried,' I reply.

'We have also had our troubles. You have heard?' I nod. 'They were looking for me as you told me they would.'

'They will return,' I say, and a look of pain crosses his face. 'This time they killed only ten. How many do you think they will kill next time?'

'I know what you are trying to do,' he says. 'You cannot provoke me to do what I do not wish to do. If I leave this place it will be because I have decided it is best to do so, not because you have goaded me.'

'The Japanese will keep looking until they find you,' I say.

'And even if I leave this place they will still look,' he says.

'They have spies along the river – they will see us as we pass. They will know you have gone.'

'These people do not wish me to go,' he says. 'To them I am many different things – they depend upon me.'

Our eyes meet and I can sense something different in his expression – a look of supplication, almost as if he were begging me to stop.

'Perhaps you are right,' I say. 'Perhaps the Japanese will not come back. That would be better.'

'Yes,' he says, but he does not sound confident.

Johnson looks like a wild man. His hair is matted and he has a scraggly, unkempt beard and smells even worse than he did on the boat coming upriver. All day he sits in his room, brooding. He curses the woman who brings his food and he curses the children when they pass his room. Nance and I have both tried to talk to him, but it has done no good. He has only one thing on his mind.

'When are we going to leave? We've waited a month already. You want to wait until the Japs come back? Is that what you and the spook want – to get us all put in one of those POW camps?'

'You're talking crazy, Johnson – you know that. It's not going to help things.'

'You and that nigger – if it wasn't for you, we'd be outta here right now, back on the ship – away from these savages.'

'And if it wasn't for you, Montgomery would still be here and alive instead of rotting in the jungle somewhere.'

Johnson glares at me, eyes narrowed with hate. The emotion is incandescent, and I remember the yellow eyes that followed us in the jungle. At this moment Johnson is like that animal, except that he's more dangerous because he's more cunning.

'We're leaving when I say,' I tell him. 'Things are working out now. Be patient!'

'Fuck you and your nigger patience,' he growls.

I go back to my room and lie down. There is nothing left to do except stare at the ceiling and wait. Everything is ready – it all depends on the priest. The first part of the trip downriver should be easy enough, but the last half will be a different matter because by then the Japs will know what we're up to. We'll need luck then.

There is a sound outside my room and Nance steps in. I nod to him and he sits down, with his back braced against the wall.

'I've been talking to the people, Captain – they're scared. They say that the next time the Japs will kill them all.'

I study his face. There is a look of real concern on it.

'I don't think that'll happen, Nance. What good would it do the Japs to kill all these people? They want the priest, that's all. They don't give a damn about these people.'

'That's just it,' Nance says. 'These people mean nothing to them. They'll shoot them down like animals. They did it before and they'll do it again.'

'There's nothing we can do about it,' I say.

'These people are innocent, Captain – they don't have anything to do with this war.'

'Look, Nance, you don't have to convince me – I'm not one of the guys who wants to shoot them. Those guys have yellow skin and slanted eyes. I'm just a poor slob doing what he's told to do.'

I shouldn't be so sarcastic, but something inside has snapped and I don't care anymore. I'm tired of hearing about Nance's troubles and Johnson's troubles and the priest's troubles. I just want to complete the damn mission and get the hell out of here.

Nance looks at me for a moment then falls silent and stares at the ground.

'I'm sorry, Nance,' I say. 'I'm tired that's all – I want to get this thing over with. I know how you feel about these people. I don't want to see them killed either. But the only thing we can do is try to persuade the priest to come with us. Once he's gone the Japs will leave these people in peace.'

I offer him one of my home-made cigarettes, and he takes it and lights up. We both smoke in silence. The sound of laughter and kids playing comes to us from outside.

'What are you going to do when the war is over and you go back to the States, Nance?' I ask.

He shrugs. 'I dunno, Captain. Before I was drafted I worked in a factory that made lamps. It was a lousy job but it paid a buck. I'll probably go back to it if the job's still there. What will you do? You got a job that pays a million a year lined up?'

Nance is grinning at me now.

'I'm a teacher, Nance – teachers don't make a million a year.'

'You don't look like a teacher, Captain. Most of my teachers were old ladies with false teeth and faces that looked like they just bit into a lemon.'

I laugh and we smoke some more. Outside, the day is heating up and we both feel lazy.

'Johnson looks bad, Captain – you figure he'll make it?'

I shake my head, a gesture that might mean 'no' or 'I don't know' – I'm not sure myself what I mean.

'If things get tough he'll crack,' Nance says. 'I've seen guys like that before. At Guadalcanal, I was in the platoon of a guy who flipped out. Started talking to himself. We complained but nobody would do anything about it.'

'What happened in the end?' I ask.

109

'The guy stopped one in the Solomons.'

'Front or back?'

'It was a mortar shell – blew him in half.'

'So that nobody could tell which direction it came from,' I say.

'You ever serve in a unit commanded by a nut, Captain? Do you know what it's like to see your friends turned into raw meat because the guy who's giving the orders isn't playing with a full deck?'

I pass him another cigarette. It has become quiet now. People are sleeping through the midday heat.

'What if the priest won't come, Captain?'

'He'll come.'

'The longer we wait, the harder it's gonna be to get outta here. All the Japs got to do is watch the river.'

'We'll get out, Nance.'

'You know, Captain, this reminds me of something that happened to me once when I was a little kid. In the summer my mother used to send me down south to a place in Alabama called Pickensville. My grandmother lived down there – she had a little farm. Summer in Newark is hell, so when school ended my mother would put me on a Greyhound bus and when it stopped my grandmother would be waiting for me. I loved it down there – used to play in the woods, hunted squirrels and rabbits, went fishin'. I had a great time. I never wanted to leave when fall came and I had to go back to Newark. I used to cry and holler – once I even tried to hide in the woods and my grandfather had to come looking for me. Boy did he lay into me – used the same switch he used when he was drivin' his mule team.' Nance chuckles. 'Going back to Newark was like goin' back to hell. All the dirt and the smoke, the garbage and the winos and the prostitutes. Man, I hated to go back.'

'This isn't Alabama, Nance. We're in Borneo and the island is swarming with Japs. If they catch us they'll probably torture us . . . before they kill us.'

'Japs, rednecks, wop gangsters . . . I can't see much difference, Captain. I been dealing with people like that all my life.'

Now we can hear the children outside again. They have finished their nap and are going to the swimming pond. They stop in front of our long house and call Nance. He finishes his cigarette then rises to leave.

'Take it easy, Nance,' I say.

He gives me a peculiar look.

'Don't get yourself all worked up. You don't want to get like Johnson – that won't do anybody any good.'

'You don't have to worry about that, Captain,' he says; then he smiles. It is a simple, toothy smile, but there is something reassuring in it that I need and am more thankful for than I could ever tell him.

It is late afternoon and I am dozing when the priest comes to see me. From the expression on his face I know that he is unsettled, but when he begins to talk his voice does not betray this. It is noncommittal, calm, as if I were one of his parishioners and he were paying me a visit.

'You seem to have regained your health,' he says. 'I am glad to see that.'

I watch him without answering.

'Your friend is in the swimming pond. That seems to be his favourite place.'

'Nance can stand the sun better than I can,' I say.

'I had not thought of that,' he says with a gentle smile. 'Here one hardly notices that sort of thing, but at first I could not bear the sun for more than half an hour. I suffered terribly.'

I don't reply and there is a silence that we both feel increasingly awkward. But I will not make it easier for him. We have waited too long already.

'You have been with us a long time,' he says, now looking away. 'Your superiors must be concerned.'

I shrug and again there is silence.

'What will your superiors say when you return without the object of your mission?'

'I don't know,' I say.

'You're an American,' he says. 'They will be angry but they will understand. If you were a Japanese it would be a different matter. Of course that is the difference between the two sides in this war. I understand it very clearly. In other things they are the same but in a matter such as this there is a difference.'

'An important difference,' I say.

'This I understand,' he says.

'And yet you will not leave,' I reply.

'What purpose would it serve?' he asks, gesturing with his

hands, and for the first time I notice how Italian he looks. 'I have told you all that I know, and if I leave this place there will be no one else to send out messages. You will gain nothing.'

'If you stay the Japanese will capture you,' I say. 'They will force you to reveal the code that you use. That will make it possible for them to intercept messages.'

'Why do you think I would be so weak as to tell them the code?'

'They have ways,' I say. 'You yourself know this.'

He looks uneasy now, but I do not think that what I am saying worries him. The code is not important enough for him to risk his life for, and chances are the Japanese know it already anyway. He must know this.

'This game wastes our time,' he says. 'We both know what it is that concerns me: the people in this village. They are the ones I am responsible for, not the code or the war, not you and your men. It is these people – they are my flock.'

'The Japanese will come again,' I say. 'They will keep coming until they have captured you or killed you. As long as you remain in this place these people will be caught in the middle – they will be slaughtered like sheep. The only way you can stop this is to leave.'

'You prophesy doom,' he says. 'I do not choose to think in that fashion. I have lived in this place for a long time and I will continue to do so. Your war is not my concern. My life is in this place – I have no life outside of it. Do you expect me to change my life because of the wishes of men whom I don't know for reasons which I do not believe in?'

I wait for a minute before answering him. I want my answer to sound reasoned, even calculated. I want him to think that I have thought long and hard about this problem, that I *know* what has to be done.

'You can bring the woman with you,' I say, then wait for his reaction.

There is a tremor, a slight flush that shows he is reacting to my words, but quickly this is replaced by a sardonic smile.

'That would not be possible,' he says. 'Here I make my own rules, but once I leave I cannot do this – once I leave I must be as all priests are.'

Now it is my turn to smile.

'Your flock!' I say sarcastically. 'Your responsibility! Why do you tell lies to yourself – it is the woman who keeps you here! If

112

you leave you must leave her behind. You would sacrifice the lives of these people because you fear the censure of your church and society!'

I can see the anger flare in his eyes. He damps it down, but I know I have hit a nerve. A man can lie to himself, but when the truth is put before his eyes by another it is hard to avoid it. Anger comes first but later there is recognition.

'We can talk no more,' he says. 'I am a patient man but you provoke me.'

'I did not think that you could lie to yourself like this,' I say. 'I thought you were a man of greater integrity.'

He turns abruptly and steps through the doorway, and I lie back, wondering if I have gone too far this time.

The rest of the afternoon is a blur. I doze and wake and doze again. Thoughts of home keep running through my mind. I have been gone from the ship for nearly two months, from my family for almost two years. I have missed them before but never so much. It must be the village and watching the kids and the women. On ship I did not feel the same way. There I was surrounded by men, most of whom were feeling what I was feeling. But I am alone now and I am sick of the war and sick of worrying and fighting. I want some peace. I want to read a book and see a movie, have a quiet meal with my wife and make love. I remember the strange, sheepish smile she always wears in bed, like a kid who's doing what she knows she shouldn't do but also knows she'll enjoy. That's her charm – there is something impish about her. I can remember her shoulders and her breasts and her hips . . . the small cherry-coloured birthmark on the back of one of her thighs. God, I'd like to be out of here! Hurry up, priest! I think. Please hurry up and do what you know you have to do!

Suddenly there is a scream and the sound of people running, then the *rat-tat-tat* of machine-gun fire. I scramble to my feet and dash towards the porch. People are running around madly, women calling their children, children screaming in fear. Already I can see people fleeing into the jungle. Then the sound of machine-gun fire comes again.

Nance is standing at the edge of the jungle, waving to me. I scramble down the log stairway and run towards him. The *rat-tat-tat* comes again and bullets zing over my head. Then we are in the jungle, running as fast as we can. Bullets fly over our heads and we can hear screams all around us. The Japs are

113

following us, firing as they go, shooting anyone they can get into their sights.

The forest thickens and we slow down.

'What are we going to do, Captain?' Nance asks.

'Wait, then go back,' I reply. 'They won't stay forever. My hunch is that they'll do just what they did last time – look around, search the fringe of the jungle, then return to their base, wherever that is.'

'They'll never catch the priest that way,' Nance says.

'They don't expect to,' I answer. 'They want to flush him out. If they make things difficult enough, raise enough havoc and kill enough people, then the Kelabit will deliver him into their hands – at least that's what they think will happen.'

'But these people will never do that,' Nance says. 'They love this guy. They'll never drive him out.'

'We know that but the Japs don't,' I say. 'They don't understand the psychology of these people – they think everybody's mind functions like theirs.'

'Then they'll just keep killing more and more people and nothing will happen,' Nance groans.

'There's only one way to stop them,' I say, 'and that's to convince the priest to come with us. Once he's gone the Japs won't bother with the village anymore.'

'Why won't the guy go?' Nance asks.

'It's the woman,' I answer. 'He won't go without her and he can't go with her.'

'For a piece of tail!' Nance says. 'These people are dying because that priest won't give up a goddamn piece of tail!'

XIV

The forest is clothed in darkness, but overhead the moon has risen, filling the night with pale silver light. When we reach the edge of the forest we will be able to see across the clearing. If the Japanese are still in the village we will see them.

Nance is just ahead of me. He has had a hard time holding himself in check. For three days we have been waiting in the jungle; already on the second day he wanted to come back to the village, but I would not let him. Now, as we approach, I can almost feel the excitement in him. I am not so eager. I think I know what we will find and it will not be pretty.

Now we are at the very edge of the clearing. Beyond lie the two swimming ponds, then an open space, then the porch of the long house with the log stairway going up to it. The scene looks peaceful enough with the water of the ponds glinting in the moonlight and a soft breeze rippling the leaves at the very tops of the trees.

Nance steps out of the forest and starts across the clearing. I tell him to stop, but he ignores me and continues on.

I stay in the shadows and watch. When he reaches the stairway below the porch he pauses and looks around. I can see him clearly from the edge of the forest even though the distance is almost a hundred yards. He ascends the stairway and vanishes into the long house. Several minutes pass before he reappears on the porch and calls to me.

I hesitate. If this is a trap, we have fallen into it perfectly; taken the bait. And now, if I enter the clearing, we will be hooked with no hope of escape. There is a noise to my right and I crouch down. A figure emerges from the forest and steps into the moonlight: a woman carrying a child in her arms. She advances towards the long house and I see others following her, coming now from all around the clearing. There must be a hundred of them – men, children, old women. They walk mechanically, as if they were drifting in a dream.

I stay in the shadows for five more minutes; then, while the last of them is climbing up the log stairway to the porch, I step out into the open and start across the clearing.

Already I can hear sounds coming from the long house – nothing distinct, no words, but an unending, wailing moan.

Inside the long house there is a peculiar, sweetish, sickening smell. A few people move about carrying torches that cast a flickering light.

Bodies line the hallway. Some obviously died where they fell; others had tried to crawl back to their rooms. The floor is covered with dried blood. Everywhere there is whimpering and crying. A few people are still alive but these too are very near death. Groups of people hover around, trying vainly to rouse them to life. The priest moves from group to group, inspecting the dying, then shaking his head and moving on.

Nance is standing alone, leaning against a pillar and staring into space; his eyes are glassy.

I try to help the wounded but it is useless – if we had penicillin and morphine we might be able to save a few of them but without medicine there is nothing I can do.

The stench becomes overpowering, and I go out to the porch to clear my head. The breeze has picked up now and all the leaves are fluttering. Behind me the moaning has stopped and in its place is an unnerving and depressing silence. One or two survivors come out from under the archway, carrying bodies. Soon others follow, and I watch as they cross the clearing and walk towards a place at the far end. Here someone has spread straw mats and the bodies are laid on them. Already some men are constructing scaffolds that will support small platforms, each for a single body. When we first entered the village I noticed one of these, supporting the decaying body of an old woman. The villagers will cover the bodies with earth and leaves to stifle the odour of rotting flesh, but it will be months before they are buried.

It is long after midnight, but the people work steadily until the long house is cleared of bodies and the hallway swept and purified. Just as they finish and the last body has been raised to a platform and covered with leaves, the rain starts, a few drops angling down in the wind; then, a minute later, a steady shower. I want to stay outside on the porch because the smell of death is still strong in the long house, but the breeze has picked up and I begin to shiver so I go inside.

Nance is where I saw him last, almost an hour ago, still leaning against the wall like a man suffering from catatonia. When I approach he looks at me but says nothing.

'I've never seen anything like this,' I say. 'They killed as many as they could.'

'But they didn't get who they wanted,' Nance says. 'They didn't get us and they didn't get the priest.'

I don't reply.

'All because a guy won't give up a piece of tail,' says Nance. 'Priest!' – his voice has risen now and it echoes down the hallway – 'You killed these people, priest! Do you hear me? You killed them and we helped you!' Then he begins to weep.

XV

I am sitting in a shady place at the edge of the clearing, watching the people move back and forth across it. The clearing seems empty even though it is mid-morning, the time when everyone is usually out of the long house. A few children are swimming and some women are grinding rice into a kind of pulpy mass which they will use to make cakes. Over half of the villagers were killed in the raid, all those who could not make it to the jungle before the Japanese reached the clearing. We have heard the story now from those who saw it happen.

Twenty Japanese soldiers came out of the jungle. No warning was given because they had killed the sentries. Boys hunting for birds at the edge of the jungle saw them and tried to cry a warning. The soldiers shot them but the noise of the gunfire was at least a kind of alarm – it enabled many of the villagers to reach the safety of the jungle. Had this not happened more of them would have been killed.

The soldiers ran into the clearing with their guns blazing. Some of the villagers sought shelter in the long house, but the soldiers sprayed the building with machine-gun fire then entered, shooting all those who were still alive. Then they pursued the Kelabit into the jungle, but after a short while gave up the hunt and returned to the clearing where they remained for a day and a night, waiting to see if any would return. The ashes of their campfire can still be seen. They slept in tents and did not enter the long house again even though they could hear the cries of some of those within who were dying in agony.

On the afternoon of the second day the Japs left, going off in the same direction they had come from – to the north, over the

Tamabo Mountains. Men who were watching the clearing saw them go and followed them through the jungle.

These men say that there is a camp of Japanese soldiers in the centre of the mountains, a place where giant silver birds land. They say that it is four days' journey to this place, and that the river near it is guarded by Japanese soldiers. I ask them how many men stay in this camp, but they do not know – only that the number is large.

Nance has spoken little since the first night. I see him often, walking through the long house or lounging in the clearing. Sometimes he swims with the children – those who remain. He laughs when he is with them but otherwise his expression is solemn. The priest, I have seen even less. I know that he is still in the long house, for I have seen him enter and leave it, but he has not spoken to me. The priest's woman was wounded in the attack but she escaped into the jungle. She is not fully recovered, but her wound was only superficial and she will survive. Those people who remain, the survivors, seem unchanged. They act as they did before, laugh, hunt and fish, seemingly unworried about the future. Only the mothers of those who were killed are different. Often I see them standing at the top of the clearing, near the scaffolds that support the rotting bodies, their faces streaked with tears.

It is afternoon and the sun has moved high overhead shrinking the shadows, so I rise and walk back to the long house. Two women are walking a little before me, a woman of perhaps fifty and a younger woman who looks to be her daughter. In front of them is a small boy of six or seven. The boy looks back as he walks and smiles at me.

At the bottom of the log stairway that leads to the porch we must wait while a man descends; then we start up. The women and child go before me. I am halfway up when I hear the old woman's voice. She has already reached the porch and is out of sight, but I can hear her berating someone. Then I hear the younger woman's voice – she seems to be trying to calm the old woman down.

When I reach the porch I see the old woman standing off to the side, tears streaming down her face; the younger woman is talking to her and stroking her arms the way these people do when they comfort each other. Near the doorway stands the priest, a peculiar expression on his face, not embarrassment but something akin to it. There are several other people on the

119

porch; they are all staring at the old woman, but now and then they twist their heads to look at the priest.

The old woman starts to talk again – apparently her daughter's attempts to soothe her have had little effect. She is staring at the priest and her words come faster and faster; then she breaks into tears and the younger woman leads her away into the long house.

The silence that follows is unsettling. The priest has not moved; his head is twisted so that he can watch the old woman and her daughter walk up the hallway. The other people on the porch are staring at him. They look confused and uncertain. Something important has happened; I don't understand exactly what but I have a good hunch.

After a minute the priest moves to the log stairway and starts to descend. Just before his head disappears below the edge of the porch our eyes meet. I have seen that helpless, pleading expression in his eyes before, but it was never so intense. He knows that the moment he did not want to think about has come. Don't worry, baby, I say to myself, Mama's gonna take you home.

The evening has come and it is peculiarly peaceful and beautiful. A soft breeze stirs the leaves and I am standing on the porch, watching the sun set. The people have eaten and are outside, spread around the clearing, standing in groups, talking. The young girls are flirting and, every once in a while, a couple sidles towards the side of the clearing and disappears into the shadows of the forest. The children, playing a game that looks like tag, rush madly about. The insects have not started their evening serenade yet, but a few of the small white birds with scarlet-tipped wings that usually stay in the depths of the forest are flitting back and forth across the clearing, twittering cheerfully. Nance joins me.

'It's not exactly like Newark is it?' I say.

He grunts a kind of agreement.

'Do you ever wonder how the war is going, Captain?' he asks me.

'Nope,' I say. 'I never think about it, Nance. It wouldn't do any good anyway, would it? Whatever will happen will happen. I just do my part, that's all.'

We watch the kids play for a while. One of them, a little

fellow with big, almond-shaped eyes, stops beneath us, looks up at Nance and smiles, then rejoins the game.

'You know, Captain, if there were more people like these and less people like Johnson and Montgomery, there wouldn't be so many wars. Did you ever think about that?'

'A lot of people have thought about that, Nance, but I don't think it has ever made much difference.'

'You think that if the people who make those big decisions – the people in Tokyo and Washington – could see these people here like this they'd still make wars, Captain?'

'I think you're being sentimental, Nance,' I say.

But Nance isn't convinced.

'Doesn't make sense to me, Captain. I can't understand why people would start them if they really understood what happens in a war.'

'Nance – you figure people understand what it's like in Newark? Do you figure people know how bad it is there?' The questions seem to confuse him and he doesn't reply.

Then, after a few minutes, he says, 'I don't know, Captain. I never thought about it much.'

'Well take it from me, Nance – people know what it's like in Newark. Maybe they don't like to think about it, and maybe they even have a special kind of mind that keeps them from thinking about it, but most people know.'

'I don't get you, Captain – I don't see what Newark has to do with this place and the war.'

'It's evil, Nance – evil is what I'm talking about. Everybody knows it exists but nobody does much about it. In fact, I'm not even sure people should do anything about it. Maybe it's all part of the big plan. If there weren't wars maybe people would reproduce so fast that they'd cover the earth like ants.'

Nance shakes his head – he's not buying.

'I ain't never been to fancy schools like you, Captain, and I ain't read all those books you've read, but I know what's good and what's bad. My grandmother used to read the Bible every day, and she used to say "We gots to praise the Lord and fight the devil." This war's the devil, Captain.'

We fall quiet again. The sun is almost down, and the sky to the west is a brilliant crimson that shades to rose then emerald then cobalt blue overhead. I offer Nance a cigarette but he doesn't want it.

The Kelabits begin to file past us as they return to the long house for the evening. The sound of their voices rises and falls, a strange, bird-like singsong.

'When do you think the Japs will come again, Captain?'

It is what we have both been wondering for the last few days.

'No way of telling,' I say. 'Could be next month or next week or even tomorrow.'

'But they'll come, won't they, Captain?'

'Yep,' I say. 'They'll come.'

We turn and start towards our rooms, but before we step through the archway a man appears. He says nothing, merely waits in the shadows.

'It's the priest,' Nance says softly.

The priest remains in the shadows when we pass under the arch not six feet from him; then, when we walk down the hallway, he follows us. At the entrance to his room I bid Nance good-night and go on to mine. Before I step inside I turn to see if the priest is still following. He is standing a dozen feet away, staring at me.

'Do you want to speak to me?' I ask.

He shakes his head and smiles sadly. 'You have won,' he says.

Almost the entire village has come to see us off, climbing down the path behind the waterfall and spreading themselves around the lake. A few have followed us into the cave where the boat is tied up. It is difficult to see in the darkness and for several minutes, until our eyes have adjusted, we stand like blind men. Above the water is thundering down, but here there is a hushed quiet; I can hear men breathing. Then slowly things begin to come into focus.

The Malay has already boarded the boat and is storing the food we are taking with us. Johnson had climbed aboard and is sitting in the stern, waiting to be transported back to the world he knows. Nance and I are still on the outcropping of rock that projects into the water like a small pier. And behind us are the priest and his people. They hover around him, helpless, mute – looking as if their god is leaving them destitute. The priest is speaking to the elders, delivering final words of counsel in hushed tones. Later I will ask Nance if he understood any of what the priest told them; now it is not important.

The Malay says something and I nod to Nance and we step

aboard. The boat rocks gently in the choppy water. The Malay has already loosed the ropes, but the current, lapping against the rock, holds us in place.

'How long we going to wait for the priest?' Johnson asks. 'We don't have all day – tell him to hurry up!'

I sit down on the deck with my back braced against a crate. The Malay is fooling with the engine. I can't see Nance, but I guess he's probably doing what I'm doing. This is something we can't rush.

I wonder what the Kelabit are thinking. They have no idea of the world we are going to – to them their priest is vanishing into the great unknown. Their world consists of their valley and the surrounding forest, the Iran Mountains, and the upper reaches of the Kayan. Beyond is a dark void, out of which come, from time to time, men with uniforms carrying weapons that spit death. Other than this they know nothing of the world to which the man who has counselled and doctored them, who for ten years has settled their quarrels and listened to their worries, is going.

The people around the priest are touching him, as if by so doing they may keep some of the magic he possesses. All the people inside the cave are men – the elders and middle-aged men of the village. They form a tight knot of bodies around him; then they separate and through them walks the priest's woman. No one speaks to her but they make room for her beside the priest. Now the voices of the villagers begin to rise as they bid him a final good-bye. He steps aboard with the woman and nods to me, and I tell the Malay to start the engine.

It makes a great roar in the confines of the cave. Slowly we back out, pass under the waterfall, and move out onto the small lake, turning as we do so.

The people of the village dot the shore. They stand without speaking or gesturing. The Malay guns the engine and we move towards the end of the lake where the river exits. The priest is standing at the stern, watching the people. Now there is another noise mixed with the chug of the motor and the roar of the waterfall – a long, drawn out moan, a sound of infinite sadness. I twist towards Nance.

'They are calling him,' he says. 'They're calling his name.'

The priest stands like a statue, watching his people, his features a stone mask except for the eyes, from which tears well and flow down his cheeks.

XVI

All through the day the boat chugs steadily down the river. Nance and I take turns at standing guard. I don't trust Johnson with the rifle. The priest and his woman sit under the canvas awning, watching the jungle glide past. She has never left the village before and is frightened, but the two speak little. Although the priest is not wearing a clerical collar, he is dressed in a dark-coloured shirt and trousers. The woman is wearing a sarong that has been dyed a rich purple. It highlights the red-brown of her skin and her shiny black hair. Close to her on the boat, I am acutely aware of her beauty – she is a striking woman and would be so anywhere in the world. I wonder how the priest will introduce her when we reach the coast and are picked up.

Johnson is grumbling already. Before, he complained because we did not leave; now he complains because the priest's woman has come with us.

'It doesn't matter,' I tell him. 'What are you worrying about? We'll reach the coast in four or five days. Inside of a week you'll probably be back in the States. What do you care?'

'We didn't bring any goddamn woman up the river and we shouldn't be taking any down,' he says.

He looks worse than ever. Red spots discolour his sunken cheeks and fever burns in his bloodshot eyes. He is wearing the same clothes he began the journey in; they are stained and greasy and haven't been washed since we were put ashore. It is difficult to sit or stand near him because he smells so bad.

The Malay sits in his chair by the wheel, steering us carefully down the centre of the river. We have not hit the long, straight stretch yet – the place where we were attacked on the way upriver – but it is on everybody's mind. I can see the Malay's eyes sweeping from side to side, anxiously studying the forest, wondering when a party of warriors, their faces painted white, or a Jap patrol will appear. Nance is doing the same, a rifle cradled in his arms. Johnson is crouched in a place that he has constructed for himself near the bow – a small fort made of boxes and crates where he feels safe.

We are moving at a good speed now and there is the feeling of a soft breeze that is refreshing. The river is as smooth as silk, the same rich, dark brown everywhere. I have seen a few crocodiles and one monkey, but otherwise nothing living except the people on the boat.

We round a bend, and suddenly I realize that we have come to the straight section. Nance crouches down and clicks off the safety on his rifle. The Malay guns the engine and we move faster.

It is late afternoon and the sun is low on the horizon behind us, throwing our shadow large on the smooth water. The trees line the stream here like sentinels. There is a scream to our left and Nance raises his rifle: a monkey, hanging out of the trees, is berating us.

The river passes the great, tree-covered bluff where the two branches merge then curves to the east. Nance looks at me and nods, as if to say 'Well that's past.'

The sun is sinking fast now and monkeys then deer and wild boar begin to appear as they come down to the river to drink. There is still a little bit of light in the sky behind us; then it is gone and the darkness is total. We are descending fast and will reach rapids sometime during the night, but it is impossible to tell just when because our speed is much greater than it was when we came upriver. The rapids will make a great roar that should be sufficient warning for the Malay to stop in the quiet stretch at the head – to try to shoot them in the darkness would be suicide.

I lie back and stare at the sky. It hardly seems possible that we are on our way and that somewhere a hundred and fifty miles to the east a boat will pick us up. Now everything that has happened to us seems like a dream, but a strange, nightmarish dream that no one would believe. I look towards the far side of the space beneath the awning – the priest and the woman are sleeping there. They lie side by side, the priest on his back

125

staring upward and the woman on her side, her face pressed into his shoulder. She is sleeping but I do not think he is. Like mine, his mind is probably too full for sleep.

I hear a faint roaring sound, leap to my feet and go to the bow. The river is widening out into a small lake and beyond, on the far edge, lies the first set of rapids. I signal to the Malay that we should stop here for the night and he nods.

We glide towards the shore, and Nance scrambles out and loops a rope around a tree; then the Malay steers us to the centre of the lake, drops an anchor over the side, and finally crawls under the awning. Soon I hear him snoring.

I am beginning to grow drowsy. The night is absolutely still and the heat, which I did not feel so acutely while we were moving, falls over me like a smothering blanket. The roar of the rapids is steady and oddly comforting. It drowns out the other sounds of the night, the eerie moans and shrieks from the jungle and the never-ending hum of the chorus of insects. Just before I fall asleep I hear the distant hoot of a hunting owl, echoing forlornly over the water.

Nance is shaking my shoulders. I sit up. It is still pitch dark. I can see the Malay crouching and peering at something beyond. Then I hear the calls – three hoots – just like the sound I heard before falling asleep. Only this time they are much louder and are answered by hoots coming first from the opposite side of the lake and then behind us. The hoots behind us sound close – not more than forty or fifty yards away.

'They have us surrounded, Captain,' Nance whispers.

'Tell the Malay to start the motor,' I say. 'We'll shoot the rapids and make a run for it downstream.'

Nance whispers to the Malay and indicates with gestures what he wants him to do. The man does not move.

'No dice,' Nance says.

'I'll have to do it then,' I say.

'Let me do it, Captain,' he replies, but I shake my head.

'You're a better shot than I am. Wake up the priest and Johnson. Three guns are better than one.'

I stay low and make my way quickly to the motor and the crude pilot's wheel. I have seen the Malay start the engine countless times but I can't remember where the switch is. If I could use a flashlight it would be easy, but that would give us away and I would be a perfect target. So I fumble in the darkness, groping for something to turn or pull.

After what seems like several minutes, I find a knob. I turn it but nothing happens. Again I search and still nothing. The hoots are increasing in frequency and they seem louder now: our only hope is movement. If we remain stationary, even with three men firing rifles, we will be taken easily.

Suddenly it dawns on me that I should pull the knob. I do this and the motor turns over. The hoots now come one after the other, loud and almost frantic. I pull the knob again and the engine starts.

The engine races when I pull the knob out farther, but still we aren't moving.

'Hurry up, Captain!' Nance yells. 'I can see something moving out there!'

The Malay appears from beneath the awning and moves to the side of the boat, releases the rope that ties us to the tree on shore, grabs a chain and jerks it, then begins to reel something in, hand over hand . . . the anchor.

We shoot forward and I spin the wheel and head towards the centre of the rapids. The moon has gone behind a cloud and I can see nothing. Even in daylight the task would be difficult, requiring experience, skill and no small amount of luck. In the dark it will be next to impossible.

A white line appears ahead and the roar grows; then we are over the edge, shooting through foaming water. The boat twists from side to side, then lists to the starboard and it seems certain that we will turn over. I hear a grating noise, as if we were scraping along a great piece of sandpaper. It lasts for only a second or two, but those seconds seem like eternity.

And then we are through into smooth water and racing ahead. I shout to Nance, telling him to check for breaks in the hull. There is no time to stop. If we can pass through those rapids in the dark so too can the men who were encircling us.

Several minutes pass, during which we chug full-steam ahead, Johnson and the priest standing at the stern, rifles in hand, the woman crouched down in Johnson's makeshift fort.

The Malay takes the wheel and I go to help Nance. Together it doesn't take us long. There is a place amidships on the starboard side where the planking of the hull, already old and rotten, has been battered and scraped so that the spaces between the boards are leaking water at a rate which will sink us inside half an hour. We call Johnson and the priest and they begin bailing. Meanwhile, I look for something to stop the leak.

The best thing I can find is a piece of old canvas that probably once served as the original awning. It is patched and full of holes, half rotten, but when we stuff it into the spaces between the planks it reduces the leak to a trickle. How long it will hold out the water we can only guess; once completely soaked through the old canvas may give like a sieve, but for the moment at least we are watertight.

I go to the stern and take up a position beside Johnson and the priest. We can see nothing behind us, but the night is pitch-black and it is possible that there are canoes out there that we don't see. Nance joins us. I want to take the gun from Johnson but don't know how I can do this. The priest is holding his rifle awkwardly, as if it were a loaf of bread; Nance takes it from him and he goes back to his woman. Johnson watches him go.

'If it wasn't for that damn priest and his whore nobody would be chasing us and we wouldn't have anything to worry about!'

'He's the reason for the mission, Johnson,' I say. 'He's why they sent us here.'

Johnson swears and looks back out across the water into the impenetrable darkness.

'Dayaks or Japs, Captain – which do you think it was?' Nance asks.

'Dayaks,' I say. 'We've heard that call before. Japs would have fired at us.'

'Do you think they'll follow?' Nance asks.

'No way of telling – Dayaks don't like to leave their own territory, but we don't know where the boundary of their territory is, and if we're still inside it we're fair game.'

'Savages!' says Johnson. 'Crazy fuckin' savages!' He is still holding the rifle, and I watch his hands; his trigger finger is twitching. He would love to shoot somebody and I don't think it matters who.

The air is heavy and humid and mosquitoes buzz about our heads. The smell of the river is strong here – a wet, muddy, living smell that seems to carry with it the spirit of all the creatures that swim through this river and live near it – the crocodiles and snakes and leeches and fat, carp-like fish. We can sense them gliding beneath and beside us, waiting, living on and on, generation after generation as they have for a million million years. We are interlopers in this world – we do not belong here, and if we make one false step this world will rise up and swallow us forever.

'We got another rapids coming up, Captain,' says Nance. 'And the next one is bigger.'

'Two more, Nance – two more but the next one is the bad one.'

Nance remembers – this was the place where we had to burn the leeches off him. He probably still has some scars.

'By dawn?' he says.

'About then,' I say. 'No reason for everybody to wait up all night. We'll take turns standing watch. I'll go first. After two hours Johnson replaces me. After Johnson you go.'

'What about the priest?' Johnson asks. 'He's got eyes like the rest of us.'

'I don't trust him, Johnson,' I say. 'Do you want your life in his hands? He's been around these people too long.'

Johnson has no answer to that and I wink at Nance.

When Nance wakes me to replace him the sky is already streaked with pink. I smoke a cigarette and watch the sun rise. The Malay is steering between catnaps, and the others are asleep beneath the awning.

The sun draws the first steam from the water that had cooled during the night and the animals begin to appear to drink. Already I can feel the heat beginning to grow. The engine coughs then resumes its steady *chug-chug*. I wonder how much fuel is left. This would not be a very good place to run out. Soon we will hit rapids again, long, treacherous rapids that the boat was unable to climb through when we were ascending the Kayan. We won't have that trouble now, but whether we will be able to control the boat in the rush of water is another matter. If we spin out of control and capsize we will be stranded. To walk out of this jungle would be impossible. No one would ever even find our bones.

I flick my cigarette into the water and take out another and am just about to light it when the Malay's cry stops me. He has seen the rapids before I have even heard them, but now, as I listen, I hear the faint roar and can see, far ahead, the low-hanging clouds of spray and mist.

129

Nance is already out from under the awning, standing at the Malay's side.

'He's worried, Captain,' he says. 'He's not sure we can make it.'

'We don't have a choice,' I say.

In only a few seconds the roar has become deafening. The others have risen and are all standing in the bow, looking at the white water which begins about a hundred and fifty yards ahead and seems to continue forever. The Malay has the engine full-throttle in reverse but he is having trouble holding our position.

'That water looks pretty rough,' says Johnson. 'You sure this piece of junk can make it?'

Nance shoots a glance at him but says nothing. The woman is at the priest's side. She looks amazingly fresh and rested, calm, more beautiful than ever. Of all of us she seems the least concerned.

'We ought to tie down everything we can,' I say. 'It's going to be rough.'

Systematically, we move over the boat, pushing boxes and barrels together and binding them as best we can with the old, half-rotten ropes that lie in big coils in the bow. When we have finished this, each person takes a seat amidships, his back braced against the bulwarks. There are no life jackets.

I signal to the Malay, he pushes the throttle forward and we shoot towards the rapids. Nance has twisted his head to watch what happens. Johnson does the same for a few seconds then looks away. The priest begins to pray and the woman sits beside him, an expression of calm on her face that is uncanny.

Then we are in the spray and the boat begins to buck and twist and leap like a bronco. It's a world of foam, air and water mixed into one, and everywhere, overpowering all senses, the crashing, ceaseless roar of the water as it pounds its way over rocks and between the narrow banks of the river. Nance has joined the Malay at the wheel and together they struggle to hold us on course. The wheel seems to have a life of its own, spinning first this way then that. Nance is a strong man but even he can't control it, and I crawl towards the bow to help him.

Visibility is zero. If there are rocks in our path there is no way to steer around them anyway. All we can do is try desperately to hold the boat on course and pray that our luck holds.

Suddenly the wheel loses all tension.

'The rudder's gone!' Nance yells.

We spin like a top. Water is everywhere, pouring over the deck. For a minute I am convinced we have gone under and grab the wheel to keep from being swept away. I hear shouts but can't see anything.

And then we are floating in a tranquil pool just below the rapids. The roar and the cloud of mist lie behind us, and all is bright sunlight and the glint of morning light on calm, glass-smooth water.

The Malay is beside me, clutching the wheel like I am. Nance is stretched out, half-drowned, an arm hooked around the base of one of the posts that support the awning. The others are still aboard, Johnson coughing and cursing and looking like a drowned rat, the priest and the woman locked in each other's arms in the stern.

Nance retches and vomits about a quart of water. We both look back at the roaring cataract. As we watch, a log, nearly as long as the boat, is spun through the air and tossed almost thirty feet where it disappears in the foam, only to reappear a minute later, floating just ten yards from us, the white of the wood showing where the bark has been torn and gouged by the rocks.

'Now I believe in miracles,' Nance says.

'It must be our passenger,' I say, nodding towards the priest. 'He probably still has some pull with his boss.'

Nance looks at the priest who is bending over Johnson, trying to help him stop coughing.

'I hope you're right, Captain,' he says, ''cause I got a feeling we're gonna need all the help we can get.'

The Malay puts down the anchor and Nance dives over the side to inspect the damage. The rudder is not gone, but one of the cables that run back to it has snapped, and we have no spare. We could splice the wire with rope but that will not last very long.

'There's only one more set of rapids to shoot,' I say. 'After that it won't matter – if the rope breaks we can stop and replace it.'

Nance doesn't like the idea.

'It could go at any time,' he says. 'And when it goes we'll lose control and be completely helpless.'

'Whadda we waiting for?' Johnson says. 'The longer we stay

131

here the closer whoever is following us gets. Fix the damn rudder and let's go.'

'He's right,' I say. 'We have to move on.'

Nance searches through the coils of rope stored in the bow of the boat until he finds one that has not begun to rot and then goes overboard. A half hour later we are underway again, chugging steadily down the river. Johnson is back in his fort and Nance is sunning himself to dry off. The priest has joined me at the bow while the woman works at the Malay's stove, preparing some food.

'Safe for the moment at least,' I say.

The priest nods but does not remove his eyes from the jungle. He seems to be searching for something but what I can't tell. The expression in his eyes is haunted, as if he were a man going to his doom instead of one returning to civilization after a decade in the Stone Age.

'How much time will it take us to reach the coast?' he asks.

'Three or four days,' I say. 'Unless we meet with more problems.'

He says nothing and continues to stare at the forest as we slide past. Two crocodiles slither into the water and follow in our wake, cruising smoothly, their snouts raising furrows.

'How will you rendezvous with your forces when this boat reaches the coast?' he asks.

I tell him only what he needs to know – that they will be waiting for us.

'But the Japanese forces patrol the coast – surely an American ship cannot have remained in coastal waters all of this time.'

'The coast is long,' I say. 'The Japanese do not have many ships here – they must use them for other purposes. There's fierce fighting in New Guinea and in the Marianas; most of their ships are there. Already they are spread too thin.'

'Yet they have many men on this island,' he says. 'They hold Kuching and Jesselton and Tarakan.'

'Their men are wasted,' I say. 'They have spread them throughout the islands and in Burma, Thailand and China. They've tried to conquer the entire Pacific and in the end they will have only a handful of ashes.'

'You sound confident,' he answers. 'Thus far they are still the victors.'

'It won't last,' I say. 'It'll take time but eventually they will be defeated.'

I study his face. We have been discussing the war, but he does not care about the war. It has driven him from the village where he wanted to stay, but beyond this it does not matter to him.

'You think hard thoughts, my friend,' he says suddenly, as if he can read my mind. 'I am no patriot.'

'Then why did you help us? Why did you send the radio messages?'

'This is a question I have been asking myself,' he says. 'Perhaps I was a fool.'

'Men do not risk their lives for a cause unless they believe in it,' I say. 'You speak as if the war means nothing to you but I do not believe you.'

He raises his hands and opens them, as if to say 'Who knows?'

For a few more minutes we are both silent; then I ask him the question that has been in the back of my mind since I first came to the Kelabit long house.

'Why do you want to stay in this place? It's not the woman, although she's beautiful. And you yourself said that the people are not Christians and that you no longer try to convert them.'

'I told you the reason,' he says. 'I am needed. The people depend upon me.'

I shake my head. 'That is not the reason. You do not stay because of the needs of these people. You are a good man but you are not a saint. Something else holds you.'

'You have been too long in this place,' he says. 'You imagine things.'

'It's not me who has been here too long,' I say.

But he does not reply, and after a moment Nance calls me and I join him amidships. The canvas we stuffed into the spaces in the hull is no longer holding the water back, and already it is three or four inches deep. I pick up a bucket and begin to bail, while Nance goes to find more old canvas. The priest remains in the stern, staring at the jungle.

During the afternoon the others sleep while Nance and I stand guard. The leak has been reduced so that it is manageable; with constant bailing we will remain seaworthy. The situation is not good, but with luck we can manage until we reach the coast.

The sun has almost set when we come upon the final rapids.

133

This descent is easy, and we take it in our stride. Now that we know the coast is near, two or three days at most, all of us except the priest are beginning to relax.

The boat passes through a stretch where the river is so still that it is almost impossible to detect the movement of the water. Everything is gilded rose-gold by the dying sun and the silence is profound, broken only by the haunting cry of an unseen bird. We round a bend and suddenly the Malay cuts the engine. Extending across the river directly ahead of us is a solid wall of canoes manned by men whose faces are painted white. And in the centre is a canoe from which extends a pole holding something that looks like a scarecrow. It is only when we have drifted almost to a stop, not more than twenty feet from the canoes, that we realise the scarecrow atop the pole was once a human being. It takes a minute more before we recognize the features of the scarecrow.

'Jesus!' says Johnson. 'Jesus-H-Christ!'

The thing on the stick was once Montgomery. How long ago that was there is no way of knowing. I want to look away but I can't. The body is shrunken and dried, the muscles and sinews knotted like old vines. Montgomery's fatigues still cover the loins and chest, but the bottoms of the trouser-legs and the sleeves of the shirt have either rotted or been torn away. The body is impaled, and what looks like the sharpened head of a spear protrudes above the throat. I hope he was dead before they did that.

But it is the face that holds me. The eyes are hooded but open, staring; the expression is unnerving – that of a fanatic, fixing us with his scalding, righteous glare.

The men in the canoes are silent and motionless, their eyes black and snakelike in whitened faces. There are at least fifty of them.

Nance edges towards me, rifle in hand.

'Don't shoot!' I say.

Behind him I can see Johnson crouched down in his fort, his rifle protruding above the top of a crate as if he were in a foxhole.

I call to Johnson, but there is no response. I think I hear a click – the safety! he's clicking off the safety on his rifle!

'Get the rifle from him!' I say. 'Do it any way you can but get it!'

While all this happens the men in the canoes do not move.

Their expression remains unchanged. Their eyes are glittering and keen, yet they do not seem to see us. The sensation is odd: fifty men looking at us and yet not looking. Then I realize why – it is not us they seek. They have not come for the Malay or Nance or me: it is the priest they want.

And now he comes forward and stands in the bow of the boat and begins to speak. I watch the men in the canoes – their eyes are fixed on him, they seem to drink in his words. What I am watching is not a priest speaking to his flock, but a messiah talking to his followers.

When he has finished speaking, a canoe glides over the water and stops beside us. The priest looks over his shoulder for a moment – I can see his eyes rest on the woman – then he steps into the canoe and it is rowed back to rejoin the others; then, without a word, the canoes all move off down the river and around a bend and they are gone.

Nobody speaks for several minutes. Finally Johnson starts a stream of curses that runs on without stop. Mixed with the other obscenities are the words 'fuckin' savages', said over and over again like a litany.

The woman is staring off down the river in the direction in which the canoes disappeared. Her lips are moving, forming words, almost chanting them. At first I think she is using the words of her people, the strange, bird-like language of the Kelabit, but then I realize that, although the rhythm and intonation are alien, I have heard the words before: it is the 'Apostles' Creed' that she is saying.

XVII

The chorus of insects have begun their nightly song; mixed with this is the whine of hungry mosquitoes. We are in the lowlands now and there is no wind to blow them away. The woman and the Malay have retreated beneath the awning. Nance and I are standing a painful lookout.

The moon rises and for a few minutes it is visible, a dull orange ball just above the horizon; then a thick mist drifts in and with it low-hanging clouds and darkness. Yet the night is not black; instead there is an eerie, pearl-like iridescence in the air.

'Did you hear it, Captain?'

Nance's voice is soft as if he is afraid he will be overheard.

'Yes,' I say.

'Drums?'

'I don't know.'

The sound is mingled with the whine of the mosquitoes. It seems to grow louder then dies down again.

'What are we going to do, Captain? We can't wait here for long – the Japs have got to be looking for us.'

'We can't leave without the priest,' I say. 'Tell the Malay to run us into shore. We're going after him.'

'Into the jungle?' he asks in an incredulous whisper.

'It's the only way.'

The Malay runs the motor only for half a minute; then we drift close enough to shore to wade in, the water lapping around our waists, and slip into the jungle. We each have a rifle and a dozen rounds of ammunition. Nance carries three grenades – the last of our supply.

We stay close to the river, where the trees are farther apart and there is some visibility, and slowly work our way downstream. At first we hear only the songs of the insects, so loud now that we are in the jungle that they obliterate the other sound, the one we are listening for. But gradually, as we move farther and farther downstream, we pick it up again: a chant, growing soft then loud then soft again.

The river turns to the south and we follow it, staying just within the covering edge of the forest. The moon is still hidden by clouds but the mist that hangs over the river has thinned.

The sound is loud now and we stop; we do not want to stumble into their midst.

Crouching low, we inch forward. I can see a glow ahead, the red of a fire tinting the trunks and foliage of trees about thirty yards ahead of us. My heart is pounding and my mouth dry.

'You go right,' I whisper to Nance. 'I'll go left. Wait until you hear my signal – two shots – then use the grenades. Don't be sloppy!'

'A lot of men are going to die, Captain.'

'There's no other way,' I say. 'Do you want to end up like Montgomery?'

I move off, crouched low, separating the leaves and branches carefully as I work my way along the river-bank. The chant is louder now, a strange, discordant wail I have heard before.

I reach the edge of the trees and part the leaves. The Dayaks are squatting in a circle; in their centre a fire is burning, its flickering flames turning the white paint on their faces red.

The priest is standing before the fire. He seems to be going through the motions of saying mass. The Dayaks follow his every gesture, their voices rising and falling in that weird chant. He raises his hands towards the dark night sky and they strike their breasts; again, then once again. The priest moves through the ceremony like a man entranced, his features fixed in an expression that is almost ecstatic.

Suddenly the Dayaks fall silent, and the priest turns his back, reaches into the fire and lifts something out. He raises it over his head and chants in Latin:

> 'Accipite, et manducate ex hoc omnes:
> Hoc est enim corpus meum.'

When hhoc est enim corpus meum.'

When he turns towards the Dayaks again his face is changed: the

137

fierce almost joyful expression has faded and now the eyes stare dully ahead and the mouth sags open. Slowly he lifts the thing he has taken from the fire and takes a bite from it; then he hands it to a man in the circle, and I watch as it is passed round, each man taking a bite. I know what they are eating even if everything inside of me does not want to know, because now I remember where I have heard their chant before – it was while I was halfway up the side of the crater and the white-faced men below me were dining on human flesh.

Mechanically I raise my pistol and aim at the man closest to me. I am not a good shot but the distance is less than fifteen yards. I pull the trigger and watch, half in amazement, as the face registers first surprise then fear and pain. He falls forward so that he is lying with his face on the ground before I re-member that the signal was two shots and fire once more, wounding the man beside him in the shoulder. Then Nance lobs a grenade and there is an explosion and a dozen men are lifted into the air and flung ten feet backwards. Men leap to their feet, grabbing knives and blow-pipes, but before they can collect themselves Nance throws another grenade. This one explodes directly in their midst. One man's face is half blown away; the arms of two others are nearly severed. Panic sets in and the men run for the cover of the jungle, leaving the wounded and dying behind.

Nance was accurate. Neither grenade came within forty feet of the priest, and he is still standing, a dazed expression on his face. I reach him before Nance and take his arm and begin to pull him into the jungle.

'No!' he says and jerks free.

Nance is beside me now. I look at him, but he makes no move to help. Then I hit the priest with all the strength I have. The punch is a roundhouse blow that comes up from my waist, and it snaps his head back, knocking him unconscious. I lift his body over my shoulder and move into the jungle without saying a word. As I work my way between the trees I can hear someone moving close behind me. It's probably Nance but I can't be sure.

In less than fifteen minutes I reach the river-bank opposite the boat and call to the Malay. It seems to take him forever to get the motor started. Nance has joined me now, and we wade into the stream and lift the priest aboard then climb on to the deck. Johnson and the woman stare at us as if we were ghosts. I shout at the Malay, and he starts the motor and steers the boat into midstream.

'They'll come after us,' I tell Nance and Johnson. 'We'll have to make a run for it.'

The boat shoots forward. The current is strong here, steadily flowing towards Tanjungselor and the Celebes Sea beyond. Nance and Johnson crouch down on one knee, supporting their rifles on crates. The woman has pulled the priest under the awning and is trying to revive him.

Then they come – sooner, much sooner then I had expected.

A canoe shoots out of the darkness at the side of the river and is on us almost before Johnson and Montgomery can fire. Two Dayaks manage to scramble aboard. I go for the first. He faces me, knife in hand, crouched like a leopard ready to spring. The tip of his knife is reddened with the same poison the Dayaks use on their darts – even a nick and I'll be paralyzed and helpless.

The man lunges towards me. I fire and the bullet catches him in mid-air, smashing into the centre of his chest and lifting him up as if it were a giant, unseen hand. He falls in a heap then, incredibly, struggles to his feet and lurches towards me again. The second shot hits him in the forehead and spins him off the deck and into the smooth, black water that is receding behind us.

Nance and the other Dayak are rolling on the deck. The Dayak is smaller than Nance, but he has twisted himself around Nance like a vine. In one hand he holds a knife; Nance has him by the wrist. They roll over and over, the man holding the knife and Nance holding his wrist. Nance batters the Dayak against the deck but he remains twined about him. The Dayak is clawing at Nance's face with his free hand. I want to fire but I am not a good enough shot to risk it. Suddenly the man jerks his knife hand free; almost simultaneously a shot rings out, his arm is shattered and he rolls off Nance with a moan.

His rifle still smoking, Johnson springs from behind his fort and pushes the man into the water with his foot. I hear a noise behind me and twist around. The priest is sitting, propped up by the woman. He is pointing towards the jungle and muttering something I cannot understand because the words are in the Dayak language.

Two more canoes appear, looming out of the darkness directly ahead of us. They remain stationary, holding in the current about forty feet apart, too close to the river-bank for us to avoid their crossfire by going directly towards one of them.

I order everybody to lie flat. Darts come in a swarm, peppering the water and the boat like needles of hail.

In a moment we are past the canoes and safe, swinging around a bend that turns the river to the south. Then the boat suddenly veers towards the shore, and I see the Malay slumped over the wheel.

Nance and I both leap for the wheel, reaching it at almost the exact instant when the boat strikes bottom in the shallows and sticks fast in the mud. We race the engine but it has no effect. Nance and I dive into the water and push, but we cannot budge the boat.

I order Johnson to gun the engine while we push, but he won't leave his fort. We push until our shoulders feel crushed but manage to move the boat only a few inches.

A cry comes from the boat, and we see the woman pointing back up the river. A half dozen canoes have appeared, looking like great black crocodiles on the moon-silvered surface of the river. They are still about five hundred yards away but are coming on very fast. I yell to Johnson again, but he does not move.

Suddenly the engine coughs then speeds up. We heave again and the boat slides free and shoots out into the current, pulling us behind it.

Nance scrambles aboard first then pulls me up. Johnson is still behind his barricade. The priest and the woman stand at the wheel; she is supporting him as he steers the boat.

XVIII

The river is smooth now and we begin to see mangrove trees. Once we are nearer the coast they will dominate and everywhere will be swamp. There will be more trouble then. Before we had the Malay to guide us but now we're alone.

Nance and the woman are trying to revive him but it doesn't look like he will make it. Three darts struck him, two in the shoulder and another on the side of the face. His breathing is very fast and shallow and his face is pale; it looks as if he is going into shock. From here on, Nance and I will have to steer the boat.

Inside of an hour it will be dawn; we will be vulnerable then. Because we're so close to the coast there are bound to be Jap patrols; probably from the air but maybe even by boat.

The priest is still dazed. I wonder if he understands what he was doing back there in the jungle in the night – I wonder if there is any way that a civilized man could understand that.

Just before dawn the Malay dies. There is no last minute struggle for life: he merely stops breathing and his eyes open and stare ahead into eternity. I never knew him really; he was part of the mission, just like the boat that carries me and the gun that I hold – an instrument. I should feel some sadness but I don't. I'm too tired and too worn: I only want to finish things – that's the one feeling that I have left.

When the sun rises we discover that the water has turned a muddy brown. The river is wider here, the trees are shorter with openings between them where there is swamp or tributaries running into the main stream. No longer is the jungle a lush green, instead it seems almost sear and the leaves of the trees are edged with brown.

The river widens, and we are floating on a small lake, houses on stilts on our right. The people are awake and we can see them staring at us from the doorways of their houses. We passed this place coming upstream: Dayaks chased us and Montgomery shot some of them. They must remember us and what happened before, for this time no canoes move out to intercept us, and in a few minutes we have crossed the lake and are gliding downriver again. Here the stream is narrower and the jungle seems to reach out, almost touching us. We see several large crocodiles asleep on the river-bank. Upstream, most of them were about six feet long, but here they are at least twelve feet and a few seem even longer than that. Soon we will enter the coastal swamps, tomorrow at latest. Already I am beginning to dread that. Now we know roughly where we are and that we are moving towards a destination. Once we enter those swamps things will be different. The swamps are a maze of twisting and criss-crossing waterways, without landmarks to help a man find his way.

More houses come into view, sitting on stilts on the shore. People peer down at us as we float past. We are so close to them that we can see their features clearly. Life must be harder here than in the interior, for many of these people are little better than skeletons.

The current is strong and now the boat raises a wake as it ploughs ahead. Sometimes there are cuts through the trees, and we can see far off. There is still a channel to follow but water is everywhere.

Johnson stands up and peers off towards the east; then he points in that direction and says something I can't understand. I ignore him and shut my eyes and try to sleep, because I know that once night falls and the mosquitoes start feeding sleep will be impossible.

Nance's shout rouses me: 'Zero at ten o'clock!'

Even before I have leaped to my feet and grabbed for my rifle I can hear the high-pitched buzz of the zero's engine and the *rat-tat-tat* of the wing guns.

We dive to the deck as the plane passes over us, banks, then starts towards us again. This time the pilot's aim is better, and we watch as the splashes made by the bullets in the river advance towards us; then there is a *chunk-chunk* sound as they slam into the deck.

Again the plane zooms overhead and Nance and Johnson turn, firing futilely. The plane banks sharply, makes a tight circle, then comes on again, wings glinting in the sun. This time all the bullets plough into the boat, splintering wood and ripping the canvas awning to shreds. Then the plane is gone.

We stare after it until it is a tiny pinhead on the eastern horizon. Miraculously, no one has been hit. The boat is scarred but almost all the damage was done above the waterline, and we are still sailing smoothly.

'That guy will report our position. We're like sitting ducks. We gotta change course!' Johnson whines.

I shake my head. 'We have to reach the coast. If we get lost in the swamp we'll never get out.'

'It's that fuckin' priest!' Johnson screams. 'They're hunting him, not us!'

'If you don't like the way things are going you can leave and try it alone,' I say. 'We'll let you off right over there.'

I point to the bank where the trees, covered with grey moss, reach almost down to the water. Half the leaves have dried up and the black, twisted branches make the place look like something out of a nightmare. The river-bank is lined with half a dozen crocs, sunning themselves.

Nance laughs. 'Go on, Johnson. Why don't you try it alone? A tough Reb like you can make it.'

Johnson mumbles something then goes back to his fort.

Twice more during the afternoon we hear planes in the distance, but they do not approach us. Either they are on another mission or they cannot spot us. We seem to be moving eastward, but the channel twists and turns and sometimes we are actually sailing west. Everything looks the same here so there is no way to know for certain if we are still on the main channel.

'I don't know how the Malay did it,' I say. 'There is nothing to mark a passage with.'

Nance is staring off into the swamp. Suddenly he turns and tells me to cut the motor.

'The channel is back there, Captain – behind us. We just passed it.'

We turn around then move slowly upstream.

'There!' Nance says, pointing.

I peer into the shadows but can see nothing but more trees and the glimmer of water.

'The big tree ten yards in – about five feet above the waterline – there's a notch.'

Once he points it out I can see it clearly: a gash in the bark that lets the white wood of the trees show, almost like a roadsign in the darkness of the swamp.

'I've been sighting those since just before the plane buzzed us. There's one every two hundred yards.'

The channel narrows as it takes us into the heart of the swamp, and we glide under branches and scrape against submerged roots. Swarms of insects buzz around our heads, and once we pass so close to a branch holding a sleeping python that we can count the bluish spots on its tawny skin.

Then the channel broadens and we are in sunlight again, following a path that curls eastward through a trackless area of grey, dying trees with bare branches.

'This isn't good, Captain,' Nance says. 'They can sight us from the air too easy. We better lay up until nightfall. The channel is broad here – I'll be able to follow it in the moonlight.'

I don't want to stop, but he's right so I let him steer us back into the swamp, and we tie up to a tree and try to fight off the mosquitoes.

The sunset turns the sky crimson; then darkness comes suddenly. When the moon appears we slip out into the channel, Nance turns the engine on and we head downstream. The water is as smooth as glass and the moonlight gilds the edge of our wake with silver. There is even a soft breeze blowing from the east, caressing and cooling us.

'We can go until dawn,' Nance says. 'Then we should hole up again. Two nights and we'll be on the coast.'

The night is so beautiful that it almost seems a sacrilege to mar the silence with words. Even Johnson's smell has gone, blown behind us by the soft easterly breeze.

'I hope the Japs don't have a post on this channel,' I say. 'Otherwise we'll never make it.'

'You gotta have faith, Captain,' Nance says. 'Wasn't that what you told me?'

We hear the voices of the priest and the woman. It sounds as if she is pleading with him. Sometimes her voice is humble, almost supplicatory; then she lashes out in anger, then falls silent.

Nance flicks his cigarette into the darkness. Somewhere nearby, a bull croc bellows as he searches for a mate and from across the river we hear an answering bellow and a loud splash as a croc rolls into the stream.

'This place is a regular lovers' lane,' says Nance.

We decide to cut the motor and drift with the current so that if there is a Jap patrol nearby they won't be able to hear us. Our speed is slowed by half but still we are moving steadily.

'What's the first thing you're going to do when we get back, Captain?' Nance asks.

'Make Johnson take a bath,' I say.

Nance laughs. At the edge of the river another bull crocodile roars.

'Looks like those big guys like that idea, Captain,' he says. 'Johnson's smell is even gettin' to them.'

'Let's hope the Japs on patrol all have colds,' I say.

XIX

By dawn we are in a quiet pool of water surrounded by moss-covered trees so enormous that we cannot even see the tops. Moss dangles from the upper branches in great wispy cords, and back and forth between the woollen strands flit bats and numerous tiny white birds.

The others are sleeping and I am standing the first watch. We agreed that each of us – Nance, Johnson, the priest, even the woman – will take a turn. What good all these precautions will do is problematic. If the Japs sight us from the air and the plane has bombs we will be blown to bits. A lookout will make no difference then. But we are well concealed, and it will take a very sharp-eyed observer to spot us. The real danger is the river. The Japs are liable to send a patrol boat up it. We are about thirty yards from the main channel behind a wall of rotting stumps, but a man looking closely could spot us. If that happens we will not even have a chance to flee into the forest as we did in the interior, for here there is no dry ground, only trackless swamps filled with snakes and crocodiles and quicksand.

The priest relieves me. He has not spoken or communicated with me since we brought him back except to nod when we pass each other. He knows what Nance and I saw him doing in the jungle; this is probably preying on his mind. It is easier to deny your world and its judgments when you don't have to meet its representatives face to face.

The mist rises from the river as the sun begins to heat the surface. I peer off downriver, but cannot see more than a half mile ahead. That's where they will come from if they are going to come. We should be able to hear them long before we see them. What we'll do then I don't know. All we can do is wait and hope we are not spotted.

My eyes begin to close. I struggle to stay awake because something tells me the Japs are near and I have to be ready, but soon sleep wins out.

When I wake the heat is suffocating. There are no birds or animals in sight and even the insects seem affected, for they are silent except for the occasional chirp of some forlorn locust deep in the jungle behind us.

Nance has replaced the priest on watch. He is lying in the bow of the boat beneath a makeshift awning of rotten canvas. The sun is dazzling, and from its position I know it is nearly noon; that means there are at least eight more hours of daylight left – eight hours during which we will be vulnerable.

I join Nance. He has stripped down to his shorts and glistens with sweat.

'It's too still, Captain – I get nervous when it's like this.'

He is watching downriver, so I turn my gaze in the other direction. Almost immediately something catches my attention: there is a flash of movement on the opposite bank about sixty or seventy yards upstream. Now it has stopped but I don't think I was mistaken.

I nudge Nance and we both peer upstream. Five minutes pass . . . ten. The leaves are absolutely still, the river like a sheet of glass. There! I see it again! This time two or three flashes of movement at once, as if men are inching their way towards us.

'Dayaks?' whispers Nance. I shake my head. I am certain I saw colour – the sun-bleached khaki of Jap uniforms.

'Get the others over the side!' I say. 'We're going to make a run for it.'

Nance's eyes meet mine.

'The swamp,' I say. 'It's our only hope now.'

We strike out straight into the heart of the swamp, directly away from the river, moving as fast as we can. At first the water comes only to our waists and we move easily because we're still fresh. It is almost an hour before we hear anything; then it

147

comes, echoing over the water – a dozen shots, each like the crack of a bull whip. Sound carries well in the swamp. We don't even halt. We have an hour on them – somewhere between a mile and a mile and a half distance. Every step counts now.

As we tire, the water deepens, so that moving becomes more difficult. It would be easier if we could swim, but the place is too filled with fallen logs and stumps. They lie in the water at crazy angles, forming an obstacle course. Some of the logs are rotten and crumble when we scramble over them; others are coated with mould and slime or hide snakes that dart forth at our approach, gliding off through the water with a winding motion.

After about three hours we see our first croc. This one is sleeping, resting like a giant log between two fallen trees. It does not even bother to open its eyes as we pass.

By mid-afternoon we are exhausted, and our arms and legs begin to cramp. Johnson wants to stop but fear keeps him from lagging behind. We have heard nothing behind us since the gunshots, no sound indicating that the Japs are following, but we know they are. How many is the question. They have no way of knowing which direction we struck out in and no track to follow. That means they will have split up and fanned out, a few men heading in each direction. And we can probably handle a few men . . . if we see them first.

The sun has begun to sink towards the western horizon when we hear a plane. It is still about a mile away, and we move close to a stand of trees and squat down in the shadows, with only our heads out of the water.

The plane passes over at about five hundred feet and continues on its course to the west.

'They didn't spot us!' Nance says. 'If they had, they would have come back for a second look.'

Maybe he's right – at least, it's best to let him and the others think so. But if the pilot of that plane were smart he would not have come back for a second look even if he saw us – doing so could only serve to alert us and probably cause us to change direction. Even now I wonder if we should do that. It's a gamble. A change in direction will confuse them – if they have spotted us – but it also will mean a loss of distance, and just now distance is our lone asset: every foot between us and our pursuers is to our advantage. I decide to continue as we are.

When we left the main channel it was heading east by

north-east and we struck out south by south-east. The direction is ideal. The coast south of Tanjungselor bulges out in a promontory before it turns east again. There is a headland here – wild and mountainous, the mountains going almost down to the sea. If we keep on in this direction the land will begin to rise and we will leave the swamp behind. We can make our way to the coast on that headland, then turn and follow the coast north to the rendezvous point at the southern edge of the delta of the Kayan at 2° 55′ 30″. The coast of Borneo is dotted with river deltas, and there is another at 2° 5′. The river that empties itself into the Celebes Sea there is not as large as the Kayan, but its delta and the surrounding swamps are vast. If we veer too far to the south and enter that place we will be in serious trouble. We can use the compass on Nance's watch to guide us, but everything is a gamble, and we will not know until we are nearer the coast if we have calculated correctly.

Just before the sun sets thick clouds move in, and when night comes it is pitch-black.

Johnson is complaining again. He is too afraid to lag behind but not too weak to bellyache—

'We got to rest,' he says. 'We'll drop if we keep moving.'

Then, a minute later—

'We got plenty of lead on the Nips. Nobody can follow us here. We're crazy to keep moving like this.'

'If you want to stop do it!' I say. 'Only watch out for the crocodiles.'

He doesn't answer and I can hear Nance chuckle, but the whining doesn't let up.

'If you keep it up, Johnson,' I say finally, 'I'll shoot you right between the eyes for endangering the mission. Do you get me?'

There is no answer. Johnson is behind me and he has a gun but I can't worry about that. If the Japs are close any sounds we make will lead them straight to us, and Johnson's complaints are a perfect beacon.

Sometime after midnight a croc makes a rush at Nance. He sees it just in time, leaps out of the way and it goes past him. But it turns in the water and comes back and he has to shoot it.

The sound echoes through the night. If they didn't know where we were before they will now. The sound of that shot will carry for miles.

'We have to move faster,' I say. 'Our only hope is to get more distance on them.'

But it's a slim hope and I know it. We cannot move as fast as the Japs. We are worn and weak and they are fresh. It's only a matter of time now.

There is a sudden swirl of water and Johnson screams. I can see nothing except white foam. He screams again and there are more splashes. Nance and I rush to him. A croc has him by the leg and is trying to pull him into deeper water. Its tail is lashing from side to side like a great whip.

Nance goes for it with his knife, stabbing it in the soft underbelly over and over again. The tail stops moving but the thing still has Johnson's leg in its mouth. Finally we blow its brains out with two shots and pry its jaws apart.

Johnson is bleeding heavily. We will have to stop and bandage the wound, and someone will have to carry him on his shoulders. Those shots will surely bring the Japs.

'We should have let the croc have him,' Nance says as I tighten the tourniquet. Johnson is in too much pain to reply. He lost a lot of blood and is nearly in shock.

'Don't pass out!' I tell him. 'You do that and we'll have no choice except to leave you behind.'

Nance hoists him and carries him piggyback, and we start moving again. As I walk I keep looking from side to side, watching for more crocodiles. If two attacked it's likely that more will. Apparently their feeding pattern is nocturnal, and there are at least four hours until dawn. When the sun rises they probably go to sleep, but by then we'll have the Japs to worry about.

We make it through the night, tired and scared and not knowing where we are. When dawn breaks and light comes over the eastern horizon, we reorient ourselves. We have veered in too southerly a direction, but this will be easy to remedy. The woman and the priest are still strong enough to keep going at the same pace for at least two or three more days. The problem is Johnson: Nance and I take turns carrying him, but as long as he is on our shoulders we can't make very good time. Johnson must know this because he has become very quiet. A few times we have fallen, dropping him clumsily into the water, but he has said nothing. He knows what Nance and I are thinking: that our chances would be much better without him.

All morning we move, but when the sun climbs overhead we stop to rest. The swamp is a maze of channels lined with mangrove trees. Between the channels are narrow strips of marshy land, usually infested with snakes and crocodiles. Some of these strips are covered with a thick growth of tall grass. We choose one of these places and lie down. It is impossible to sleep because of the mosquitoes and leeches and the stifling heat, but at least we can catch our breath and rest. Strangely, it is not our legs that are tired but our arms, because we must use them as swimmers do to pull ourselves through the water.

After a half hour I signal that we should continue and start to rise, but Nance holds me down. He points to the priest's woman. She has parted the grass and is looking at something we cannot see. Then I hear them. There must be at least half a dozen. They are moving briskly, splashing loudly as they come.

We lie flat and wait. Two men appear and move directly towards us. They are short and have to walk holding their rifles with their arms extended over their heads. Five other men follow behind them at a distance of about twenty-five yards. The men look from side to side as they approach.

The two leaders continue directly towards us, but the others fan out and move towards a strip of land that lies on the other side of the channel. The men do not act as if they have seen us, for they come on at a steady pace. Sweat runs off my forehead and drips into my eyes, but I am afraid to move and wipe it away.

Now I can see the men clearly. They look almost like twins, each of the same height and almost identical features. They are thirty yards away and staring directly at us. It seems inconceivable that they have not seen us, but if they had surely they would have signalled to their comrades. They must suspect that we have rifles and only maniacs would approach an armed enemy as they are doing.

Suddenly there is a noise overhead and they stop and look up. A scout plane has appeared on the eastern horizon. It comes on very fast and zooms over at a height of about three hundred feet. The men wave to it then continue on. The plane has broken their concentration, however, for they no longer are heading towards us but walk in a path that will take them past us at a distance of twenty yards. Possibly they believe that the observer in the plane would have spotted anyone hiding on this strip of land and signalled them. Possibly it is all a trick, a plan to lull us so they can take us more easily.

We watch as they move past us. When they are almost directly opposite me they stop again, and the man who is closest to me stares directly at the spot where I am hiding. His eyes glitter under the bill of his cap, and I can feel the finger which I am holding on the trigger of my rifle involuntarily tighten.

Then they continue moving and wade back into the channel. I can hear Nance release his breath with a 'woosh'.

After the soldiers have passed out of sight we wait for thirty minutes before setting off again. The patrol is downstream so we have to alter our course and head in a more southerly direction. This means we will be heading directly for the delta of the river that lies at 2° 5'. I fear that place almost as much as I fear the Japs.

The sunlight bouncing off the water is like a knife. The vegetation is sparser; the jagged branches of the trees are nearly bare here so there is little shade. A constant hum of insects fills the air, droning louder and louder like a squadron of approaching bombers. The priest and the woman, moving at the front of our short column, are soaked with sweat, and the priest seems to be struggling. We have not eaten anything besides fruit and some dried fish for a week. If we do not soon find food and a place to rest, we will collapse.

The land begins to rise. At first the grade is imperceptible, and we notice only that the swamp seems to be drying up. The ground is still covered with water, but now it only comes to a place just below our knees, and we can move faster. Johnson feels as if he weighs five hundred pounds, and Nance and I must spell each other as porter more frequently. I can see Johnson's leg. The trouser is torn away and the flesh looks as if someone has gone over it with a saw. The pain must be excruciating. I am no medical man, but I know that without antibiotics and the proper dressing that wound will fester and probably turn gangrenous.

All afternoon we trudge forward, never stopping to rest. Once Nance catches a fish and we eat it raw, each taking a few mouthfuls. As the sun begins to set at our backs the swamp comes to an end. The ground is still soft and moist but there is no more water. This means the going will be easier, but it also means we will leave tracks. If there are Jap patrols in the area they will have no trouble tracking us down.

Night comes and we keep going. When Nance and I can go

no farther, we stop. The forest has begun again, and the trees are thicker here than they were in the swamp. We tear low-hanging branches off and lay them on the ground and lie down. Immediately we fall into deep, dreamless sleep. When we waken it seems as if only moments have passed, but I notice a faint glow on the horizon ahead of us – dawn will come soon, probably within the hour.

The others are still sleeping and I have to shake them several times to rouse them. The woman still seems strong, but the priest is pale and unsteady. Nance says nothing, but he looks tired and the ribs that were once crushed by the python have begun to hurt him again. I can tell this by the expression of pain that he tries to hide when he lifts Johnson onto his shoulders.

Johnson is delirious. He rambles on about Nance and niggers and priests and me and the navy. His voice has a high-pitched, hysterical tone and carries in the swamp, but there is no way to keep him quiet. At least he is still holding on so that we don't have to tie him to our shoulders. His brain may be fogged, but the instinct for survival is still alive.

Just after the sun comes over the horizon, blinding us with its first rays, the ground begins to rise at a much sharper angle. We cannot see ahead because of the undergrowth, but it is obvious that we have begun to climb – whether it is a hill or a mountain I do not know. I try to remember the details of the countryside but I cannot. There were symbols on the briefing map that indicated uplands, but I can't recall the numbers that gave altitude. We could be entering hills that we can cross easily or mountains that will crucify us.

Johnson has been quiet for a long time and I decide to lay him down. Nance and I bend over him. His face is pale and his eyes are closed, as if he is sleeping. He is breathing fast and beads of perspiration cover his forehead. When we shake him his eyelids flutter and open for a moment than close again. The woman and the priest join us, and the priest puts his ear to Johnson's chest to listen to his heartbeat then inspects the wound. When he finishes he shakes his head.

'The infection is very bad,' he says.

'Gangrene?' I ask.

'Not yet but soon – I have seen such wounds before. Another day without medicine and the smell will start. Then it will be too late.'

I look at Nance and shake my head. We will be lucky if we

153

reach the coast by tomorrow, and there is no telling how long it will take after that to work our way north. Johnson will never make it. He has come all the way and now, near the end, he will die. I hate him but I feel sorry for the bastard. This is a hell of a place to die.

Late in the morning we reach the top of the grade. One minute we are weaving our way between tree trunks, the sun hidden by a thick umbrella of foliage; the next we are in the clear, standing on a ridge of rock that runs along the top of the hill. Before us, not more than two or three miles distant, is the Celebes Sea, glittering like a million pieces of blue glass. I look to the south. Less than a mile down the coast are the mangrove trees that indicate swamp. They extend south as far as I can see. This must be the mouth of the Berau River. To the north are cliffs and, before them, a narrow strip of sand that marks the beach. Luck has been with us. A mile or two to the south and we would never have found our way out. Now all we have to do is follow the coast north, moving at night and holing up during the day. The journey is not more than forty miles. We should be able to reach the rendezvous point in three or, at most, four days.

I am ready to let out a whoop of joy when I notice three shapes on the horizon. One of them is large, perhaps a cruiser; the other two are patrol boats. All of them are flying the Japanese flag.

XX

Night has fallen. We waited in the forest until the sun began to set then worked our way to the beach. Doing this was far easier than we imagined it would be, because paths weave back and forth over the eastern side of the hill we were on. Some of these are barely discernible; others are well-travelled. That means men frequent this coast.

Lights appear on the horizon and we stop. Japanese patrol boats! We listen for their engines but can hear nothing above the crash of the surf. The lights move off to the south and we continue moving; then they return and for a long time stay even with us, as if they are monitoring our progress.

'I don't understand, Captain,' Nance says. 'They can't see us in the dark.'

I point at the moon.

'It's almost like daylight. With a telescope they could spot us easily.'

'If they see us why don't they come?' Nance asks. 'Why don't they send a landing craft?'

'I don't know. Maybe there's a reef that they can't risk crossing in the dark – that's all I can figure.'

'So they're just keeping tabs on us then,' says Nance.

'For now,' I say. 'They've probably radioed ahead to ground forces, giving them our location so that we can be intercepted. The only thing we can do is head back inland.'

'What about Johnson?' Nance asks.

'You know the answer to that as well as I do,' I say.

Nance has been carrying Johnson and now he lays him down gently. Johnson has been sliding in and out of consciousness for

155

two days and I doubt if he understands what is happening. I reach down and shake him and his eyes blink open. They are glazed, like the eyes of a prizefighter who has just come to after being knocked out. He knows though – perhaps it is instinct, but he knows. He looks at me and laughs.

'So they finally got us, huh – just like I told you they would. We're all going to die because of the priest and his slut.'

I don't say anything.

'Give me your extra rounds,' he grumbles. 'You're a lousy shot – you couldn't hit a Jap if he was pissing on your shoes.'

I give him four clips. The pain must be getting to him, because he drops one, and when he tries to reach for it he almost passes out. I pick it up and hand it to him. His injured leg is grotesquely swollen and nearly twice as thick as the other; it balloons out his pants leg so that the fabric looks as if it will split.

'It was the crocs in the end – the priest and his slut and the fuckin' crocs. Christ Almighty who would've believed it!' He chuckles evilly. 'You better get now. You too, nigger. Take the priest and his whore and get your black ass outta here while you can still move!'

'Sure thing, Reb,' Nance says. 'Anything you say.'

We start to go, then Nance stops and looks back at Johnson. He is lying alone in a circle of moonlight. Nance raises his arm and gives him the Italian salute, one arm crooked, the hand of the other holding the biceps of the raised arm.

Johnson laughs and says, 'Same to you, champ – same to you.'

There is a new sound now; it is unmistakable – the whine of a small boat moving towards the beach.

We plunge into the forest, banging into tree trunks as we career haphazardly deeper into the darkness. Suddenly, the silence is broken by the crack of a rifle shot. There is another crack and another followed by a shriek of pain.

'They got the poor bastard,' I say.

More shots ring out, coming in a quick burst almost like a round from a machine gun. Then we hear Johnson, his voice sounding like the cry of some obscene banshee—

'Com'on you fuckin' Nips! Com'on and die!'

We begin running.

When dawn breaks we are trotting along the top of a great cliff. We have been heading north for almost four hours, staying just inside the edge of the forest. Below us, a drop of almost four hundred feet, lies the narrow strip of beach, then the sea, rough now and covered with whitecaps. A mile ahead lies a cluster of thatch-roofed buildings, and in their midst a primitive church with a steeple topped with a cross. I try to remember the map that I have committed to memory. A town lay here . . . Datumakuta, a trading village built by the Dutch.

The priest and the woman stop. They have seen the village and are waiting for me to tell them what to do. We are exhausted but more than the rest we need food, and there is only one place where we will find it. I point towards the village and we walk forward.

XXI

An old man comes to greet us. He is small and wizened and burnt cinnamon by the sun. His eyes are Chinese but his lips are fuller, his nose broader than a Chinaman's. A sarong is wrapped around his waist and extends below his knees. He stops about twenty feet from us and looks at us with interest, curious but not afraid. The priest speaks a few words of Malay to him, the strange, whistling sounds almost like music in the crystal-clear morning air.

The man regards us with interest for a minute then twists and looks back towards Datumakuta, as if he is checking to make certain of something. Apparently satisfied, he says something to the priest.

For a few minutes they talk; then the priest turns to us.

'The old man says that there are Japanese soldiers in the village. That always a few soldiers stay there, three or four, but that last night twenty more came. They arrived very late, he says; for that reason they are still sleeping.'

'Ask him if there is a way past the village,' I say, 'a path that will keep us in the jungle, out of sight of the village and hidden so that planes cannot see us.'

The priest speaks to the old man again. I watch the old man's eyes. They are alive, moving rapidly from the priest to us then back to the priest. The old man is obviously worried and knows what will happen if the Japs catch him with us, but he does not appear to be terrified. He understands the situation and seems vaguely amused by it. When he speaks again it is for a long time, with many gestures. He points to the sea and then the sky. His eyes narrow and glitter with hatred, and his voice becomes shrill. Finally he stops and again the priest turns to me.

'The old man says that the Japanese come from the sea and the air, that they fly in great planes and float in great ships. He says that they are clever and strong but that they are evil. They force the villagers to give them food and take their houses and use their women. He says that the villagers hate the Japanese.'

'Just ask him how we can get around the village,' Nance says. 'We gotta get moving.'

I nod agreement. 'Tell him we hate the Japanese too,' I say. 'Say that we go to meet friends in the north so that we can tell them where the Japanese are. Tell him these friends will return and destroy the Japanese.'

The priest speaks to the old man again. He listens, glancing back towards the village from time to time. When the priest has finished the old man squats down and scratches a map in the dust. He makes a line to show the coast and some Xs to indicate the village, then he traces a line between the village and the coast.

'Is he saying that there is a path near the beach?' I ask.

The priest says something to the old man, and he shakes his head then points towards the cliff and speaks again.

'The path is on the cliff,' the priest says. 'It is carved into the rock. Only the villagers know of it.'

'How far does this path go?' I ask.

Again the priest speaks; the old man listens intently then answers with two words.

'To the Kayan,' says the priest.

XXII

On the map the shore line looked nearly smooth, moving in a slight curve to the north-east almost without indentations until it reached the mouth of the Kayan. In reality it undulates like a snake, the path twisting and turning so often that the distance, which cannot be more than thirty miles as the crow flies, is much greater.

Sometimes we move at a brisk walk, at other times we slow to a crawl as we inch our way along, pressed flat against the face of the cliff. The path was carved into the cliff long ago and parts of it have been so eroded by the wind and rain that there is almost no foothold at all. Every hour we have to stop to rest. The lack of food is really affecting us now and we are unbearably thirsty. Here, exposed to the bright sun and salt air, our thirst grows more quickly than it did in the jungle. Already our skin is blistered and spots of light dance before our eyes. Beneath us the sea twinkles and glimmers like a million sapphires. Gulls circle above us, cawing loudly. And always there is the boom of the sea, as it swells and surges and hammers against the cliff.

The priest is fading. Before, this was hardly noticeable, but he seems to be weakening with every passing minute. If we stop to rest, sitting with our backs pressed against the cliff, he has to be pulled to his feet when we start moving again. The woman is worried. We must go single file, so that it is not possible for anyone to help him. One misstep could be fatal, and in his weakened condition – it looks as if he may collapse completely at any moment – he is in great danger of plunging into the sea. She wants to use the rope to tie herself to him, but he won't let her do this.

When the sun begins to set we have to stop. Already the path is in shadow, and it is very narrow here. We backtrack about fifty yards to a place where the path is a little wider and sit down with our backs pressed against the face of the cliff. Now that the sun has passed overhead it is cold. A breeze comes from the east, blowing the salt spray into us. Our clothes are soaked and soon we begin to shiver.

'We better use the rope,' I say. 'We can circle it once about everyone's waist. Nance will hold one end; I'll hold the other. We are still strong and can hold out while you sleep. When you are rested, you'll take our places.'

The priest nods. He is pale and his lips are twitching. The woman pulls him to her, and he rests his head on her shoulder and in a moment the two have fallen asleep.

'We need food, Captain,' Nance says. 'We need it bad. We should have gone into the village.'

'We couldn't risk it,' I say. 'One more day, maybe two. If we can just keep going we'll make it. We're safe here – the Japs will never find us. We can make it.'

'Bullshit!' Nance says. 'The priest can't go any farther and you know it. If we could carry him he might make it, but we can't do that here, and if we go back up – that's saying we could go back up if we wanted to – the Japs will get us.'

'He'll keep going,' I say. 'Sleep will make a big difference. He'll keep going.' Nance doesn't answer. We're both too weak to argue.

It is dark now and the moon, a pale silver crescent, has risen, illuminating the sea with a brilliant white light so that we can see each wave clearly. Directly below us there is a place where the water shimmers with an orange-pink phosphorescence. The scene is almost indescribably beautiful, but I am so weak and cold that it does not lift my spirits. The emptiness of the sea is numbing – it stretches on and on like a great field of silver snow. Night in the jungle was different; there I could feel life all about me – the humming insects, the cries of the hunter and the hunted. Here the emptiness is eerie and forlorn.

There is a jerk on the rope and I brace my heels and push my back into the rock until the pain is almost more than I can bear. But no one is falling – the priest and the woman are still on the ledge, still sleeping.

'You dozed off, Captain – I heard your breathing change. We better wake them. You're not going to be able to make it.'

'The woman,' I say, 'not the priest. He needs sleep more than I do.'

Somehow we get through the night. The woman relieves me and then I relieve Nance, so that when dawn breaks we are trembling with cold but rested enough to go on.

Then we have a stroke of luck. A gull alights on Nance's shoulder and he grabs it before it can fly off. In a second we have wrung its neck and devoured it raw, drinking the blood as if it were water. The uncooked flesh nauseates us but we do not vomit it up, and some of our strength returns, even the priest's.

We keep moving until sunset then stop to rest once more. The moon rises and again the sea is turned silver. In the darkness it is possible to peer far up the coast, which arches gently to the north-east. There is a line of silver where the waves crash into the base of the cliff, but then it disappears. I nudge Nance and point to that spot.

'What's it mean, Captain?' he asks.

'That's the mouth of the Kayan,' I say.

By mid-morning we reach it. The path descends gently and the sea comes closer and closer, and then the path ends and we are walking along a muddy beach. The cliff has vanished and the shoreline turned sharply west. Beyond we can see the jungle, and coming out of it, like a great muddy snake, the Kayan.

Through the steaming hot afternoon we walk almost due east, moving along the beach for several miles. The going is not easy but now we have plenty of water – there are numerous streams which come out of the jungle and cross the beach – and fish to eat. We find the fish washed up on the shore; most of them are dead and decaying, but there are crabs and prawn which are still alive and we fall on these like vultures, devouring them raw. Once Nance goes into the forest and returns with some orange berries. We have no idea what kind of berries they are, but he saw birds eating them so we know they are not poisonous.

Our morale has picked up. Nance is beginning to talk of home and the woman seems happier. Only the priest is still depressed. He is strong enough to keep up with us now, but his

162

eyes are filled with a haunted look, and from time to time he twists his head and peers towards the jungle. When he does his expression changes. I expect to see fear, for it is out of the jungle that the Japs will probably come if they track us down, but the look on his face is not fear. It is not an enemy he is looking for.

The sun begins to set and we move close to the jungle and make camp. The woman gets palm fronds from the trees and makes pallets; she wants to build a fire to roast some fish but we won't let her do this.

I lie down and stretch out. The feeling is almost too delicious. It feels as if I have not been able to do this for an eternity. In a few moments I have fallen into a deep, sound sleep.

When I awake several hours have passed. The others are still sleeping soundly. We have been reckless; there was no lookout. If the Japs had come in the night we would have been taken like helpless children.

I rise and stretch. I am still tired and could sleep for four or five hours longer, but someone has to stand watch. Using the compass on Nance's watch I calculate that we are at 2° 55', which means we must find a way to cross the river and work our way north through the islands in the estuary of the Kajan. My calculations are rough. We may have to walk for another day or we might be less than a mile from the rendezvous point. The mouth of the river is filled with small islands. On one of them there is a radio buried in a waterproof box. The location is exactly 2° 55' 30" N. We will know the island when we see it even if our calculations are off, because it is perfectly round with a ring of palms on the seaward side. The landward side is covered with bush and reeds. The water on the seaward side is shallow and filled with reefs, but there is a channel to the open sea that the Japanese are not supposed to know about. That's the channel the PT boat which will pick us up will use, but nothing will happen until we reach that island and use the radio.

The stars start to fade and the sky to the east turns pink, then rose, then orange. Nance wakens and joins me.

'You didn't get much sleep, Captain,' he says. I tell him I'll rest once we reach the rendezvous point. 'Close huh?' he asks and I nod.

'We'll probably reach it before the day is over.'

'What happens then?' he asks.

'We send the signal and wait.'

'How long?'

'No telling,' I say.

'And the Japs?'

'We just have to hope they don't decide to scout the area.'

Getting to the first island is not easy. Nance and I are good swimmers and the current is not very strong – we could probably swim across to it. But neither the priest nor the woman is a strong swimmer. We find a log on the beach. It is waterlogged and rides low in the water, but the priest and the woman can sit astride it and paddle with their hands. Nance and I follow them out.

As we move away from the shore the current grows stronger. At first the change is nearly imperceptible, but when we are fifty yards out we find ourselves struggling to keep from being swept into the open sea. Nance and I can fight the current better than the priest and the woman can. They paddle frantically, but the current hits the log broadside and inexorably pushes it towards the sea. With a frantic effort Nance and I chase after the log and grab hold of it; then, after we rest for a moment, we move to the ocean side and start kicking.

Slowly we win the battle and the log begins to move towards the island. We cannot even stop kicking for a moment, because when we do the log immediately turns in the current and moves rapidly towards the open sea again. Finally we devise a system, so that we rest, alternately, every few minutes. When that happens the log hovers in the current, moving neither nearer to the island nor to the open sea. Then, when the man who has rested begins kicking again, we start to move once more.

By the time we are halfway across we are thoroughly exhausted, and it seems impossible that we will make it all the way. My legs are cramped and each kick feels as if it is draining all my reserves. But we go on, and gradually, as we move closer to the island, the current slows and our progress speeds up.

We touch bottom on the very eastern edge of the island, in an area filled with slime and quicksand, and stumble ashore, too spent even to pull ourselves up the beach to dry land. Only when gulls begin to dive and peck at us do we find enough strength to force ourselves to our feet and totter to more solid ground.

Almost all afternoon we sleep, waking only to eat the fresh crayfish and crab which the priest's woman has prepared. When nightfall comes we make our way to the northern shore and peer across towards the next island.

Here the channel that separates the two islands is much shallower and it looks almost as if we will be able to wade across. The water shimmers in the moonlight; it is very calm, almost without waves, and Nance wants to cross immediately.

'Why wait for morning?' he asks. 'In the daylight they'll be able to spot us from the air – maybe even the shore.'

I agree and we begin to wade into the water when a shout from Nance makes me raise my eyes. About twenty yards out three shapes, like large logs, are moving towards us.

We whirl and sprint for shore. The shapes continue to lance in towards us, finally stopping only about ten feet from where we are standing. Each croc is at least fifteen feet long.

'They're looking for a midnight snack,' I say.

An hour after sunrise we start across again. The crocs have all gone back to wherever it is they go for their morning snooze, and nothing bothers us except a fish hawk with poor vision who mistakes Nance for a surfacing sea bass and rakes his cheek with its talons.

This island is like the first. The palm trees which grow at its perimeter completely girdle it. It is not the island we seek and there is no radio here. We cross it quickly and then stop on the northern shore.

The next island is not more than fifty yards distant. There are palm trees on its eastern half, but the western side is covered with bush and reeds. And the island is round – at least it looks round from our vantage point – as perfectly round as a quarter.

Nance lets out a whoop of joy.

'This is it, Captain – this is the place! We're almost home!'

The priest and his woman are standing behind us. I turn to tell him the news but there is no need. He understands well enough and he does not look happy.

XXIII

The radio is supposed to be ten yards to the west of the tree that stands the farthest east on the island. We dig through the sand like starving dogs in search of a bone and, suddenly, there it is: a crate wrapped in two layers of green canvas, beneath which is a skin of rubber. The radio is shiny and new, the batteries fresh and strong. Together with them is a flashlight. Inside of half an hour I am sending out the prearranged, coded signal. Five minutes later I receive an acknowledgment.

The rest of the day is uneventful. We find shade and lie down beneath the palms. One man stands guard while the others try to sleep. The sky is high and clear and the sun burns like fire. The island is filled with flies that bite continually, and eventually we tear palm fronds from the trees and try to use them as switches. These afford us a little relief but not much.

Night falls and a steady breeze rises, blowing from the northwest. It bends the reeds on the western side of the island and blows the sand in a fine spray that dances just above the ground. We try to sleep but none of us can. The tiredness from our journey has worn off, and now we are too keyed up, too filled with anticipation.

For a while I close my eyes and half doze, but my thoughts won't let me alone. It is as if my mind is filled with electricity. I give up and sit up. In the moonlight I can see Nance. He is doing the same, resting on his elbow and staring at the sea. From a place about twenty yards away, where the priest and the woman are lying, there is a soft murmur of voices. We are all in the same state – we know that somewhere in the dark sea we can hear roaring before us a boat is moving towards this island. We have come so far, struggled so hard and endured so much that we cannot rest. Anticipation is overwhelming us. For months this has been our goal, the sole reason for everything that we did, and now that the moment is at hand the excitement is almost unbearable.

About an hour later we sight lights. At first they are just a twinkle on the horizon to the south; then they brighten and form three distinct groups, moving steadily at a speed of twenty or twenty-five knots. They cannot possibly be from our side, for none of our ships would sail in these waters with lights.

Their motors hum faintly like a distant swarm of bees. But they get no closer, and soon the hum dies and then the lights merge into a twinkling cluster and finally vanish over the southern horizon.

The night is quiet again. The breeze has died and the palm fronds hang limp. We can hear each wave lap onto the shore.

We are still shaken by the sight of the Japanese ships, but it does not seem possible that they can stop the boat that is coming for us. The commanding officer would not be stupid enough to try to run into an island close to shore unless he was absolutely certain the surrounding sea was free of enemy craft. We know that. We believe it and trust in the wisdom of that officer and the omnipotence of the US Navy. We have to – we have to believe in something. For so long our lot has seemed helpless, the task before us so impossible, that now that we have done our part we feel it an outrage that anything could deter us from our goal. It's not logical but that's how we feel. We have come too far for some dumb, incompetent ship's captain to blow it for us.

The night wears on. Finally we sleep, almost out of boredom. The sound of the waves has become a lullaby, narcotizing our fears away and lulling us until our anxiety begins to dissipate.

I am the last to give in, and when I do so the darkness to the east is already creased by a single line of pink – the horizon, where the sea and sky meet and behind which the sun is climbing relentlessly towards us.

When I wake it is mid-morning. The sun is at 30° and the light bouncing off the waves is so intense that I have to shield my eyes. The others are near me, lying in the shade. The woman and the priest are still sleeping; Nance is trying to watch the horizon, but the glare is too much for him and he can only glance at it for a second or two and then look away.

'Maybe you should send another signal, Captain,' he says. 'Maybe they missed the first one.'

'You heard the reply,' I say. 'They got the message all right. Anything else we send out can only serve to alert the Japs. If two or three of their communications stations get a fix on us they'll be here before our side.'

Nance nods. A week ago, even a day or two, and he might have argued but not now – I can feel the difference in him. He's looking forward to getting back home. Once, for a while back in the jungle, he might have felt differently, but all of that is past – he's remembering his friends and the taste of a steak and the way his girl looks when she smiles. The good old USA may not be heaven but it's looking pretty good to him just now.

I can feel someone watching me and turn. The priest is resting on one elbow, observing me with a strange smile on his face.

'Your friend looks happy,' he says. 'You must feel as he does – safety, comfort, perhaps not the welcome of a hero but at least respect. Possibly you will receive a medal.'

'I don't need any medals,' I say defensively; then I realize that I am playing his game, slipping into the framework he has created for me. I do not have to apologize for wanting to go home. 'You do not want to go,' I tell him, 'because you want to stay where you are a blasted king among a bunch of savages. When you leave here you'll have to be like the rest of us, just one more poor slob who has to do what the rules say if he wants to survive. Here you can make your own rules . . . like God.'

He smiles broadly now, a wolflike smile that raises goosebumps along my spine.

'You have it all figured out, my wise friend. From the first you knew and everything that has happened has only confirmed that knowledge. You are a prodigy, a genius!' He flashes a look of contempt at me then peers off towards the sea, squinting into the blinding light. 'If it were as simple as that I could just remain here – I do not have to come with you, you know.'

'The Japs,' I say.

'The Japanese would never be able to find me if I did not want them to. There are two hundred and eighty thousand

168

square miles in Borneo – they hold only the coast. In the interior there are places where no outsider has ever been. I could go there and wait for this war to end. It cannot go on forever. Then I could return to my village. It would not be hard to do.'

'Do it then,' I say. 'Why don't you do it?'

'That is the question I am asking myself,' he says.

'You are deceiving yourself,' I say. 'You could never make it back to the interior from here. Even if you had the physical strength, which you don't, the Japs would catch you. It's all over – there is no way back and you know it. You chose the only real option but now, when the consequences of that choice are almost on you, you want to change it. You're living in a dream – trying to deny reality won't change it.'

'You are very certain of yourself,' he says. 'I wish I was that certain – I wish I could be that sure of anything.'

Something softens inside me.

'This place,' I say, gesturing towards the great green island behind us, 'it's a hell-hole. You can't do anything for these people. You're fooling yourself if you think you can. It's not you who has changed them – they have changed you.'

Our eyes meet for a second then he looks away.

'You are talking about what you saw back in the jungle in the night,' he says. 'Do not be so quick to judge – that is something which you do not understand.'

'Could any civilized man understand it?' I ask.

'Perhaps not,' he says. 'Perhaps no one who has not lived here . . . lived among these people . . . could understand it.'

'Cannibalism,' I say. 'People make jokes about it but when you witness it it's not a joke. These people live in the Stone Age. I guess men ate human flesh then – maybe they needed to to survive. But this is the twentieth century. You're not a savage living in the Stone Age; it's nineteen forty-four and you're a Catholic priest not some damn druid!'

He sighs.

'I could try to explain it to you but it wouldn't do any good,' he says. 'You think that these people are savages and that you – you and your friend and your army and your country – my country – are civilized. How many men have you killed? How many men have died in this war? How many are dying at this very moment? Men, women, children – they are being killed right now by other men – men who also consider themselves civilized. You call these people savages because they eat human flesh, and the very idea that men might do that fills you with repugnance. Just like you these men hunt their enemies, just like you they kill them and sometimes they are killed. And when they have killed an enemy they eat his flesh. Does it matter so much? They believe that if they eat a man's flesh they consume his spirit – that his soul and heart – his strength – become theirs. Who are we to say that idea is so wrong?'

'You don't believe that,' I say.

He laughs sarcastically.

'I have been here a long time my friend. Before the Japanese there were the Dutch and the British. They had rubber plantations which they worked with native labour. A penny a day – that was what they paid the natives. And if a native would not accept that wage – if he was a Chinese who knew better or a Malay who was too proud to kneel before his overseer – he was whipped until the white of his ribs could be seen. His wives and his daughters were taken and used and the children that the masters begot were left in the jungle for the leopards to eat. As long as the woman was young and beautiful she was kept, but when she grew old and lost her beauty she was sent away. The men who owned these plantations – businessmen who rode in chauffeur-driven cars in Amsterdam and London – grew rich off the sweat of the people on this island. They sucked their blood like leeches and threw the husks away when they were too old or too diseased to work any longer. Yet you dare to call the Kelabit and Dayaks cannibals and savages and say they are uncivilized. Do not make jokes. All men are cannibals. At least these people respect the men whose flesh they feast on.'

The woman has been listening to us. Now she rises and comes to the priest and takes his arm and leads him away. He walks slowly, like a confused, helpless child, tears streaming down his cheeks.

'I don't understand, Captain – What's he complaining about? What's the man want?'

'He doesn't know, Nance,' I say. 'That's his problem – he just doesn't know.'

Nance looks at me with a peculiar expression on his face; I don't think he believes me.

I walk towards the other side of the island, because I need to be alone where I can think. The priest has shaken me. I know what I believe – I'm no gung-ho patriot. I've thought about most of the things he said before, but I don't believe in good guys and bad guys. I know about people who ride in big cars and the people who don't have enough to eat. I know I can't do the things you have to do to ride in those cars; I couldn't make myself. I'm no saint but I couldn't sell my soul, not even if I wanted to. I've also been around long enough to know that if I want to ride in cars like that – if anybody does – he probably does have to sell his soul. Maybe I always knew this; people understand the world in funny ways, and a lot of kids know more than old geezers who have read half the books in the library.

But I was never angry about things the way this priest is. There are some things you don't want to think about too much because it won't do anything except destroy your peace of mind. Early on I learned that angry men are apt to make a lot of mistakes. I try to stay cool. No man can change the world, and you have to live in it because there's no place else to go. Sure what he says is true, but that doesn't change things. He's complaining about the world, that's all; he's moaning about the nature of things. Doing that is about as logical as complaining that the earth is round or shit smells.

Towards noon I go back to the eastern side of the island. The woman has made a meal for us from crayfish and crabs and I am hungry. The priest eats in silence. His expression has changed again; now the mask is up, and he looks calm and distant.

'When do you think they'll come, Captain?' Nance asks. He's getting nervous.

'It won't be in the daytime,' I say. 'That would make them sitting ducks for the Japs.'

Nance nods and tries to get his mind on something else. He doesn't have much luck though, and I can see him peering towards the sea while he eats.

The day wears on. The priest is sitting about fifteen yards from me, squatting oriental-fashion. When the sun passes over-head and the shadows go to the east, he doesn't move. Finally the woman goes to him and persuades him to come into the shade.

The night is calm and balmy. Once or twice there is lightning in the distance and a few drops of rain, but this passes quickly, hardly roiling the sea. There are almost no mosquitoes and the night is pleasant. Near midnight the wind begins again, raising white caps and increasing the roar of the surf. It is at about two am, just before I am due to waken Nance to take my place on watch, when I notice the light. This light is different to those we saw last night. Instead of coming from the south it seems to loom up suddenly, as if it had materialized out of the open sea to the east. And it is a single light, not a cluster. I watch it for several minutes. At first it burns steadily, but then it starts to flash. I wait a minute to be certain, but there is no mistaking it – the rendezvous signal is being sent: two long flashes, a short one, then three more long. They are out there waiting for our signal.

I take the flashlight and walk to the very bottom of the beach, stand in the shallow surf, and send the signal. It is crude but they should be able to read it – four dashes followed by two dots followed by four more dashes. To make the dashes I hold the flashlight on for a count of four, for the dots only a count of one.

The signal from the boat comes again – two long flashes, a short one, then three long.

Now Nance is at my side. He has wakened and seen the light and come to join me. He can hardly contain himself.

'They're here, Captain!' he yells, clapping me on the back. 'They've come to get us!'

We walk back up the beach to wait for them to come in. I wonder how they will do it – the tide is out and the surf is roaring. The pilot will have to be a skilful man, and he will have to know the exact location of the reefs.

'What's holding them up?' Nance asks. 'Why're they takin' so long?'

'There's a reef out there,' I say. 'They're just being careful.'

We wait, staring anxiously into the darkness. Forty minutes pass and nothing happens. Finally Nance goes down to the water and wades into the surf. The light has vanished but we expected that. Once the signal was changed there was no point in continuing the communication. But we should hear their motor by now and we don't.

Nance wades out until the water reaches his waist and stands, craning his neck and peering into the darkness. A thin mist hangs over the water, limiting visibility so that we can see clearly for only two or three hundred yards. Beyond that point the mist thickens into an opaque fog. Somewhere out there in that murky darkness is the boat that has come for us – somewhere out there are Americans like us. To know that they are so close, but that we cannot see them or hear them is maddening.

Nance lets out a sharp yell and, flailing the water wildly, dashes towards the beach. When he reaches the shore he hurls himself onto the sand and rolls over and over, screaming in pain. I rush to him.

'Jellyfish!' he yells. I urinate on him and as the stream of liquid splashes over him, neutralizing the acid poison in the stings, his screams change to moans and then whimpers. He will be swollen for days but the worst is over. I pull him to his feet.

'Don't wash it off,' I say. 'You'll have to stink for a while.'

I help him back up the beach to a place under the trees where he lies down. The priest and the woman were wakened by his shouts and join us. I explain, then nod towards the open sea.

'There's a boat out there. I sighted their signal about an hour ago, but they haven't come in yet.'

The priest says nothing. His expression is still blank – a mask that hides all feeling. The woman does not understand what is happening.

We try to make Nance comfortable and then sit down to wait. Time passes but nothing happens. My eyes are glued to the place where I last saw the flashing light, but there is nothing but the thick, pearly glow of fog reflecting the moonlight. For a while I doze, then wake, then doze again. When I look at my watch again it is four forty-five. That means only about a quarter of an hour of darkness is left.

There is a faint drone: the sound of an outboard. Almost at the same moment a dinghy appears, gliding out of the fog and heading directly for us. There are three men in it – one handling the motor, another sitting amidships, and a third perched in the prow. I give the signal with the flashlight once more. The dinghy moves forward slowly while the man in the prow peers anxiously towards us. Surely they have spotted us but they have cut their speed to almost zero, as if they are worried by something. When they reach the beach two men jump out and run towards us while the third stays at the motor.

'Let's move it!' says the first man to reach us.

Nance is already on his feet, and we turn towards the priest and the woman. The priest makes no move, so we each take an arm and begin to drag him towards the boat; he does not fight us. The woman comes along behind him.

In a minute we have waded through the surf, turned the dinghy around, climbed in and begun chugging through the waves towards the fog.

The three men who came for us peer anxiously towards the shore. Two of them are holding submachine guns; they look afraid.

We are less than a quarter mile from shore when the first rays of the sun come over the horizon, almost blinding us. I screen my eyes. Far out – the distance must be at least a mile or two – I can see the shape of a PT boat. And directly before us lies the reef, a wall of jagged rock rising up out of the calm sea. Waves are breaking against it and it is covered with foam. The reef is still about fifty yards off, but we are making good progress because the sea is calm. The closer we get, the more formidable it looks. The coral is black, covered with seaweed in places; the rocks that protrude look razor-sharp. There is no visible break in them – no place for a boat to pass through.

'Where's the channel?' I yell over the whirr of the motor.

'Hard to spot,' yells the man at the motor. 'It's only about a dozen feet wide and barely deep enough to let us through – we scraped the keel coming in.'

We have approached to within ten yards of the reef now and turn north and begin to chug along beside it.

The first shell comes before we have gone twenty feet. It was probably fired from a bazooka, and it flies over our heads, ploughing into the rock of the reef where it explodes, lifting a geyser that drenches us. I twist and peer towards the shore: in the faint dawn light I can see a dozen men on the beach and as I watch, two dinghies filled with Japanese soldiers appear from around the southern side of the island and begin to move towards us.

Shells whistle over our heads. The man at the rudder is now steering us in a weaving pattern to try to confuse the Japanese battery. More shells explode in the water, so that we seem to be sailing through a forest of geysers.

'It's not this way!' yells the man at the prow. 'We gotta turn around and head south.'

We move in a big semicircle and the shells come closer; then we are sliding along beside the reef again, weaving like a snake.

The Jap dinghies are much closer now – not more than two hundred yards away – and the soldiers start firing at us. Their bullets zing over our heads.

We find the opening in the reef and slip through and into the sea beyond. The waves are larger here and we are slowed down. The shells from the shore battery are falling short now, but the bullets from the soldiers in the dinghies are steadily getting closer. One dinghy has already passed through the gap in the reef and the other is almost at the opening.

'Can't you get any more speed out of this thing?' I yell. The man at the motor shakes his head.

The sun appears just above the horizon, almost blinding us. It is blood-red and the silhouette of the PT boat looms up against it like an apparition. We still have at least three-quarters of a mile to cover and the Jap dinghies are rapidly gaining on us. We are a clear target and only the roughness of the sea, which makes it impossible for the marksmen in the dinghies to steady their rifles, is saving us.

'Why doesn't the PT boat come for us?' I ask. 'Are they going to watch us get cut to ribbons?'

The man at the motor doesn't answer and I turn towards the other men, but their attention is fixed on the pursuing dinghies. At this distance their submachine guns are useless; all they can do is watch.

Suddenly I have a sinking feeling because I know that we are not going to make it. Almost simultaneously the shells from the shore battery begin to find the range. Then it happens – a shell hits the prow exactly in the spot where one of the sailors is sitting, tearing a hole in him as large as a medicine ball. For a second he remains alive. The expression on his face is something I will never forget: a look of surprise, as if what has just happened to him is the last thing in the world he expected. The next moment he is a crumpled heap of twitching muscle and blood and bone, and around him surges the sea, which rushes through the opening torn in the prow.

The dinghy noses down into the sea like a swimmer diving for a pearl. Nance and I swim free; the priest and the woman and the two remaining sailors go down with the dinghy. A moment later all of them bob up to the surface like corks.

The Jap dinghies are not more than thirty yards away – I can see the features of the soldiers – when the PT boat opens up. It must have begun to move towards us before we were hit, because it is in range and the first burst from its machine guns mows down half the soldiers.

But the dinghies continue on pursuing us, and the remaining soldiers crouch and open fire. At first I think they are just heroic fools firing futilely at the PT boat; then their bullets begin to pepper the water around us, and I know that they have decided to complete their mission even if they die doing it.

Nance is the first one to get hit. The bullet passes through his shoulder and he screams and flounders for a moment before he starts to sink. I grab him and hold him up, and suddenly he gives a convulsive jerk as he is hit again, this time squarely in the middle of the chest.

The priest is hit twice while I watch and the woman once in the arm. There is another burst from the PT boat and the firing stops. One of the dinghies is circling crazily, its motor still revving; the other has stopped and is bobbing up and down in the waves. Both are filled with the dead and dying – not a single man is still sitting upright. There is a loud roar as the machine gunner on the PT boat opens up for a last round, and the bodies in the dinghies dance madly. Then everything is quiet and I can feel the swells lifting me gently; only then does the pain come and with it the realization that I have been hit too.

XXIV

'You caught a pretty nasty one,' says the chaplin.

'How long?' I ask.

He looks at me strangely.

'How long till I'll be ready so they can make mincemeat out of me again?'

'Not for a long time,' he says. 'The way things look, you'll probably ride the war out back in the States.'

'Bad as that?' I say.

'Yes,' he says, 'as bad as that.'

It doesn't hurt much, but he tells me it went through the lung. I can't believe it because I felt nothing.

'That's often the way it is with something like this,' he says. 'Happens all the time in the middle of a battle – adrenalin and fear.'

This guy is young, hardly more than twenty-six or seven. He looks like one of the students who used to sit in my classes.

'You'll make it all right,' he says. 'You'll have pain for six months but you're lucky – luckier than the priest.'

I don't ask about Nance because I already know. They got his body at least and they buried him at sea. I was still too weak to go above to see him slide down into the water. Nance always hated the ocean. He hated the service and he hated the war and all he wanted to do was go back home to Newark. The poor bastard never even got a chance to do that. I want to write a letter to his family but the chaplin tells me I can't do it.

'Intelligence work can't be written about,' he says.

'So what did *you* say?' I ask him. 'What did you tell them?'

'The letter said he died while performing his duty,' says the chaplin.

'The standard bullshit,' I say. 'Did you use a form letter?'

He doesn't answer that. He's not a bad guy, a little slow but he understands how I feel. I'm not the first leader of a mission to come back with all his men gone.

'And the priest?' I say. 'How is he? Will he make it?'

The chaplin shakes his head.

'He took one through the spine and another tore out half his intestines. Must have been one of those dumdum bullets – the kind that open out when they hit.'

'How long has he got?' I ask.

He shrugs. 'A day, maybe two days. There's sepsis and peritonitis already.'

'The woman?' I ask.

'She's OK,' he says, and I notice the peculiar expression on his face. He can't quite make out what she was doing with us, and it probably seems a little strange that two of the men who were sent out never made it back but that we had room for the woman.

'I want to talk to the priest,' I say.

'He's in no condition to talk to anybody,' he says.

It is night. The orderly has changed the dressing on my wound and taken my temperature. He won't be back until early morning. The sickbay is dark and quiet except for the faint hum of the engines and the steady slosh of the waves that I can hear slapping against the hull beneath the open portholes.

I have waited for this moment. Yesterday I was too weak to stand; even now I'm still weak but I can't wait longer. There isn't much time. The chaplin told me this, but it wasn't his words that convinced me – I watched the doctor and the orderly. There's a certain way that medical personnel behave around someone who is dying. They become less perfunctory, gentler.

I sit up and place my feet on the floor. It feels strangely cold under my feet. I try to rise but my legs are too weak and I fall back down. The pain in my chest is sharp. It feels as if the wound has opened, but I can't worry about that now. Afterwards, I can ring for the orderly if the bleeding won't stop.

Again I try to force myself up. This time I succeed in standing, although I have trouble keeping my balance and have to wait for a few minutes while I steady myself. When I feel a little stronger I try a step. It works. I am feeble but at least I haven't fallen.

It takes me a long time to cross the cabin but I make it. I want to sit down, but there is no chair so I hold on to the iron bar at the head of the bed.

I can't turn the lights on, but there is a porthole just above his bed and the moonlight coming through it is falling directly on his face. He looks bad. His cheeks are sunken and his skin has a waxy look. I can't tell whether he's asleep or not, but he doesn't seem to know I'm there. I have to try and waken him. He might not come around but I have to try.

I reach down and touch his arm. At first nothing happens, but after a few minutes I notice a change in his breathing. He must be aware of my presence.

'It's me,' I say. 'It's Captain Morris.'

His eyes open and he looks up at me. The face is an expressionless mask, but the eyes are awake.

'I must talk to you.'

He moves his head an inch or so to show that he understands.

'Nance is dead,' I say. 'The woman is wounded.' I can see alarm in his eyes. 'She'll be OK – just a flesh wound. Me too. It's worse than that with me, but at least it's a ticket home.'

He tries to say something but it isn't audible. I bend over him and put my ear close to his mouth. His voice is only a faint whisper but I can make it out. He wants to know if it was worth it.

I tell him I don't know. The corners of his mouth rise as if he's smiling; then he tries to talk again and I have to bend over. He asks me who's winning the war.

'We are,' I say. 'The Japs are starting to fall back. It's only a matter of time.'

His face remains blank, and for a minute I just stare down at him. Then it comes out—

'I had no choice,' I say. 'It was the mission – a man can't say "no" when he's told to do something, not in a war anyway.'

Still his face is an expressionless, accusing mask.

'Nobody can do much about it,' I say. 'Nobody has any power – we're all victims.'

He tries to speak and I bend over him again. He tells me that now it is me who is rationalizing.

'What else could I do?' I ask.

179

His lips move to form a word that I recognize: 'Nothing.'

'You think I should have come back empty-handed – that I should have sabotaged the mission. I followed orders. That's what people have to do in a war. I'm sorry for all of this. It's not my fault but I'm sorry anyway. If I could have made it work out differently I would have but I couldn't. It wasn't in the cards, that's all.'

Now he is trying to speak again and once more I have to bend over him. He wants me to take care of the woman. He wants me to promise that I'll do that. He says she can't go back now and that somebody will have to take care of her.

I look down at him. He looks like a cadaver already, but his eyes are still alive and they have fixed me with their stare.

I nod.

He shuts his eyes. It is over.

It takes me a long time to get to my bed and when I reach it I'm completely exhausted. For a while I listen to the waves. When I twist my head to see him I can't, because a cloud has moved over the moon and light no longer floods through the porthole. A little later I fall into an uneasy sleep that gradually deepens. The next thing I know, it's morning and the room is filled with light, and the doctor and the orderly are standing at the priest's bed. From what they are doing I can tell he's dead.

XXV

'Can't be done,' the chaplin says. 'The captain says she goes into an internment camp for the duration.'

'She's not a Jap,' I say.

'It doesn't matter,' he says. 'The intelligence boys say that any natives taken from an island occupied by the Japs are to be interned. There's no way of telling who's loyal and who isn't.'

'Bullshit!' I say. 'These people were fighting the Japs – why do you think we were sent to get the priest out? Tell that to the captain.' He just shakes his head. 'What if I tell you she's my wife,' I say.

'I wouldn't believe you,' he answers. 'Neither would anybody else.'

'What other reason would there have been to bring her out?' I ask. 'Do you think she belonged to the priest?' Now he looks a little confused. 'He married us,' I say.

'Witnesses?' he asks.

'Nance and Montgomery and Johnson,' I say.

'They're all dead,' he answers.

I tell him I know that and he says he'll talk to the captain again. A little later he goes away, and a half hour later the orderly comes to change my bandage. He's almost finished when he asks me if I want to hear something funny.

'Go ahead – cheer me up,' I say.

'That guy who died this morning—'

'The priest, you mean.'

'Yeah,' he says. 'You know who he was?'

'Sure,' I say. 'A man who was fool enough to send out

181

information about the army that was occupying an island he wanted to stay on.'

'I don't know anything about that,' he says, putting tape over the gauze covering my chest. 'But his old man's a big shot. Turns out he runs the show in some town in Jersey – Hoboken or Jersey City or someplace like that. He's in politics and has a post on one of those House committees that have to do with the defence budget. Rumour has it he's a buddy of FDR.'

I ask him how he knows all this.

'They're shipping the body all the way home to Jersey,' he says. 'No burial at sea for that guy.'

I start to chuckle then break into a laugh.

'Hey!' he says. 'You do that and you'll open up again.' He finishes and fluffs my pillow then gives me a glass of water. 'Why do you figure a guy with connections like that would want to spend his time trying to convert savages?'

'Doesn't make sense, does it?' I say.

'The world's a pisser all right,' he says.

'Yeah,' I say, 'but we got fun.' He looks at me like I'm crazy. 'You know,' I say, 'like the song says: "In the mean time, in between time, ain't we . . ."'

'You're a real comedian,' he says.

The aftermath of a war game that went terribly wrong . . .

THE FIFTH ANGEL
A ONE MAN KILLING MACHINE

DAVID WILTSE

Sergeant Stitzer, said the officer who'd trained him, was a hero. He was also one of the most dangerous men ever to wear a uniform.

These days, they kept Stitzer in the cell at the end of the corridor. TV cameras watched him night and day. A broken yellow line on the floor marked the point of no return.

Five years on, Stitzer had still not surrendered. In his crazed mind he still had a mission to fulfil. And the major knew that while Stitzer had breath in his body he'd find a way to carry out those orders. And not even the most secure military hospital in the world would hold him back . . .

'Pacy, original and very readable' THE TIMES

0 7221 9107 3   ADVENTURE THRILLER   £2.95

A selection of bestsellers from Sphere

FICTION

WANDERLUST	Danielle Steel	£3.50 ☐
LADY OF HAY	Barbara Erskine	£3.95 ☐
BIRTHRIGHT	Joseph Amiel	£3.50 ☐
THE SECRETS OF HARRY BRIGHT	Joseph Wambaugh	£2.95 ☐
CYCLOPS	Clive Cussler	£3.50 ☐

FILM AND TV TIE-IN

INTIMATE CONTACT	Jacqueline Osborne	£2.50 ☐
BEST OF BRITISH	Maurice Sellar	£8.95 ☐
SEX WITH PAULA YATES	Paula Yates	£2.95 ☐
RAW DEAL	Walter Wager	£2.50 ☐

NON-FICTION

AS TIME GOES BY: THE LIFE OF INGRID BERGMAN	Laurence Leamer	£3.95 ☐
BOTHAM	Don Mosey	£3.50 ☐
SOLDIERS	John Keegan & Richard Holmes	£5.95 ☐
URI GELLER'S FORTUNE SECRETS	Uri Geller	£2.50 ☐
A TASTE OF LIFE	Julie Stafford	£3.50 ☐

All Sphere books are available at your local bookshop or newsagent, or can be ordered direct from the publisher. Just tick the titles you want and fill in the form below.

Name _____

Address _____

_____

Write to Sphere Books, Cash Sales Department, P.O. Box 11, Falmouth, Cornwall TR10 9EN

Please enclose a cheque or postal order to the value of the cover price plus:

UK: 60p for the first book, 25p for the second book and 15p for each additional book ordered to a maximum charge of £1.90.

OVERSEAS & EIRE: £1.25 for the first book, 75p for the second book and 28p for each subsequent title ordered.

BFPO: 60p for the first book, 25p for the second book plus 15p per copy for the next 7 books, thereafter 9p per book.

Sphere Books reserve the right to show new retail prices on covers which may differ from those previously advertised in the text elsewhere, and to increase postal rates in accordance with the P.O.